THE HAUNTING OF RED RIVER

MARIE WILKENS

PROLOGUE

Her heart pounded as she moved through the forest. While there was no chill in the air, goose bumps appeared on her arms, nonetheless. She couldn't explain it. The swampy land had always brought her joy and peace before. How could she not adore the estate that had been her home for so long? Meeting him was a mistake, of that she was sure. It was going to be the last time. If he didn't want to leave the area and come clean about what he'd done, she'd have no choice but to go to the law. Either way, things were going to be different come daybreak.

Moving to the edge of the rushing water, she knelt and let the icy flow move across her fingers. In the summer months, it would slow to a trickle and was the perfect temperature for an afternoon swim. Given the wet season they'd had, though, the waters were downright dangerous. The Red River that ran through the Alabama swamplands came by its name honestly.

While most assumed it was a nod to the red clay that made up the bedrock, she knew the truth. It was a place that claimed lives. Be it by accident or intent, the water called to those lost souls. A branch snapped behind her, and she spun around, wondering once again if she should flee. Instead, she stood her ground, certain they could come to an understanding as the man stepped into the clearing just feet from her.

"I didn't know you were back," he growled.

She swallowed. "Well, I wasn't sure if I wanted you to know. Some things have changed in my life, though…and I want you gone."

He chuckled, his cold gaze flickering across her body. "Sweetheart, I'm not going anywhere. Now, if you want to move on back home, I sure would like that. It could be just like it was in the old days."

Her stomach lurched. The man had abused her over and over again as recently as the year before. She wasn't a young child, scared and naïve enough to believe his lies anymore. No, she was an independent woman who had something worth living and fighting for. Glaring at her abuser, she stepped forward and lifted her chin.

"Maybe I haven't made myself clear. I am coming back home to Red River. I will be back in two weeks, and if you are still here, I'm going right to the police and my mother. I'll tell them everything about you, about what you did to me—"

His hand came out of nowhere, connecting with her jaw and sending a searing pain through her cheek. She stumbled backward, the water lapping at her rubber boots. For the first time, she felt truly afraid at the notion of what he might do to her.

"Maybe this was a bad idea," she stammered.

"Oh no, sugar, this was a great plan. I think everything is going to work out just fine in the end. We'll be one big, happy family…with or without you in it."

She stepped back again as he moved closer, his aged hands reaching out to snatch her waist. Everything that he'd been capable of in the past came flooding back to her as she screamed and tried to flee. Beneath her, the slick rocks gave way, and she stumbled just as the man's boot connected with her side. No matter how she struggled to gain her footing, the water seemed determined to consume her until, at last, the rushing waters claimed another victim.

1

Rachel could feel fatigue settling in after another successful day of filming. She had just finished a shower at the small campground where she and her sister, Becky, were staying. The pair enjoyed their time together, traveling the country in search of lost and forgotten locations. It was something they had a lot of fun with, but she also genuinely loved it. She made her living by posting the videos on YouTube and other platforms and had a little success in gaining followers. Her sister was always a little more free-spirited, but that never slowed them down.

Rachel researched new locations, and they both filmed their experiences. She spent more time in front of the camera as she talked about her thoughts on each area. They were molded out of the history of wherever they were but also her own beliefs about what made each place so unique. Over the time they had been on the road, they had seen several special and historical locations. Still, her favorite part was spending so much time with her sister. For as long as she could remember, they had been inseparable.

Having grown up in the foster care system, they really had no other choice but to rely on each other. It served to build a bond between them that was unbreakable. She quickly dried herself off and headed back to the RV. It was old and beat up, but they both called it home, no matter where they were. Crossing the campground in the middle of the night, Rachel looked up at the stars. It was another beautiful night, and the sky was clear enough to see most of the obvious constellations. As soon as she opened the door to the RV, she was greeted by her sister. Becky was already online, editing their latest video.

The location she had found was an old, abandoned elementary school just a few miles away. Though most of the places they would film had a crazy history, something about the school still creeped her out hours later. Rachel had a special ability as an empath to read the emotions of the past. The haunted locations they would visit always had a way of draining the life out of her. Still, she knew she needed to help her sister through the editing. They spent the next half an hour going through the videos they had shot, trying to find the perfect way to share.

Even as the two were watching the videos at a higher speed, the same sick feeling in her stomach came back. Most places with a dark history would do the same thing to her. She almost felt as though the spirits were trying to reach out to her or that she was reliving whatever hell they had gone through. Either way, she was drained, and the sickening feeling in her gut was coming back. Becky was the exact opposite in her beliefs. While she enjoyed the stories and working on the project with her sister, Rachel knew she didn't believe in ghosts or spirits.

They were complete opposites when it came to their beliefs about the afterlife, but she knew her sister was still by her side through it all. As they started to finish editing their newest recordings, Rachel was relieved. She couldn't wait to get out of Alabama and as far away from the school as possible. There was just something that didn't sit right in her gut, whether her sister believed in it or not.

Rachel left her sister to post the video online. She knew Becky would take care of everything after editing, and she needed a few minutes to decompress. Stepping outside, she looked up into the sky and smiled. She always had a fascination with the stars, even as a little girl. She could remember times when she had spent extra time in science classes, just marveling at all the different terms and names of constellations. It brought her a great amount of joy growing up.

After taking a few minutes for herself, she reentered the RV and worked her way back to the bedroom. She plopped herself on the bed next to her sister and smiled. Becky smiled back at her.

"So, you feel any better after looking at the stars?" Becky asked.

"I always do after a day like today."

"I'll never understand what you feel when we go to these places, but I don't mind. As long as the blog keeps growing, we'll do just fine."

Rachel chuckled. "Well, there are a lot of times I'm glad you don't have to go through the same things I do. I wouldn't wish this on anyone."

"If it makes you feel any better, the blog has over five-hundred-thousand followers. We're heading toward the big time now," Becky said. "Maybe we can actually afford to upgrade this old thing."

"Not a chance in hell. This RV has been home for too long now. It's part of the family."

Becky chuckled. "Yeah, an old grandparent or something like that. Even old people get upgrades. You know that, right?"

"I understand what you're saying, but I just don't think it's the right time to be spending money yet."

"Come on, Rachel. You do understand how having money is supposed to work."

"I don't mind spending it on what we need, but we might not have a popular blog forever, and I don't want to waste money on things we really don't have to have. Maybe after a few more successful blogs, we can do something, but we need to save some of that money for now."

Becky sighed. "That makes sense, but you promised we would slow down after the school blog."

"I know, but that's something we can talk about tomorrow."

She saw her sister roll her eyes, but Rachel wasn't

sure she wanted to slow down just yet. The idea of having to settle down somewhere and get a real job to survive frightened her. Just the thought of having to work hard for someone else to make money made her feel sick. She loved living in the RV and traveling around the country. Having to park the RV and spend money on an apartment was something she didn't want to think about for a long time. Still, for her sister's sake, she would have to consider it.

Rachel knew their blog wouldn't last forever, and they had been on a roll. She wanted to try to ride their success for as long as they could, and she enjoyed what she was doing. Becky was the wild child. Her sister loved being in the videos and editing what they recorded, but the popularity that came with it was something she wanted more than actually working on the projects. It was just another thing they felt differently about, but it didn't slow them down when it came to taking care of one another.

Suddenly, Becky jumped off the bed and moved to the small kitchen that could only accommodate someone constantly on the move. Rachel watched her sister open the cabinet and pull out three packs of ramen noodles. She smiled, knowing her twin was reading her mind. Though it wasn't the healthiest snack she could think of, they both loved their nightly noodle snack.

While her sister prepared the ramen, she sat on the edge of the bed and thought about the day's events. It wasn't any more unusual than other places they had visited, but it had left her in a bad place. She was still trying to recover from the feelings she got while they were in the school, but she tried to push the thought from her mind.

"You know, I was thinking we should invest in those things," Rachel said.

"Maybe we can just get them to endorse us, and then we'll get a lifetime supply."

"Possibly. I'll leave that for you to look into."

They both laughed at each other. Becky had dreams of living a rich lifestyle with lavish cars and big homes. Rachel had her own dreams involving having enough money so they would never have to eat ramen again. Her sister brought her the bowl of soup, and they both quickly scarfed them down. After cleaning up the dishes and telling each other good night, they went to bed. Rachel was exhausted from the day, and within a few minutes, she was fast asleep.

She had no idea how much time had passed, but she was suddenly dreaming. It quickly faded from a beautiful dream and became a nightmare as she was being held under water. She kept fighting the hand holding her, but she couldn't free herself.

Suddenly, just as she felt the last bit of air escaping and her lungs filling with water, she woke up startled. Rachel opened her eyes, still choking. At first, she thought it was from the dream, but she quickly realized she was smelling smoke. In a panic, she reached over and turned on the light. She was stunned to see the entire RV was filled with smoke.

2
───

Immediately, her thoughts raced to her sister. Rachel yelled her name. The smoke was quickly becoming thicker. It didn't take long before she saw the flames starting to climb up the walls. She knew the old RV would be reduced to ash in a matter of minutes, but they needed to grab their important belongings before they could escape. Becky woke up startled, but she understood what was happening just as fast as Rachel had.

They both made their way through the burning RV, grabbing their bags and laptops before exiting. She was happy they had both escaped with their lives, but as they stood back a good distance from the RV, all they could do was watch as their transportation and home burned to the ground. The flames were burning higher and slowly getting hotter as everything they owned—aside from their bags, laptops, wallets, and IDs—burned to the ground. The thin material quickly became fuel for the fire, and slowly, the neighbors in the campground woke up and started coming out to see what was going on.

She was still in shock, watching the RV burn. There was no telling what had started it, but that was far from her mind. Rachel moved closer to her sister and wrapped her arms around her. She knew no matter what they had lost in the fire, they still had each other. For now, that was good enough. Somewhere in the chaos of getting out of the fire with their lives and watching the flames reach higher, someone had called the fire department.

Surprisingly, they were there within a few minutes, and all the other campers started to get out of the way as they pulled their truck as close as they could. Rachel watched the team work together to attach the truck's hose to the local water source and start spraying their RV. Rachel could tell her sister was shaken. She continued to hold her tightly as the firefighters worked to put out the fire.

As with any fire, the police showed up a few minutes later and started to check out the scene. It was an amazing thing to watch them work so precisely, and if it was anything else other than their home burning, she would have been more excited to see them operate. As they watched the fire slowly die down, Rachel saw an officer walking over to them. She knew there was nothing that could be done and that everything inside was gone, but she didn't know what they were going to do next.

The officer was a young man, barely out of the

academy, judging by his appearance. He smiled shyly at the two, but the look wasn't a happy one. "Well, it looks like it's all gone," the officer said.

"Everything?" Becky muttered.

"Yeah. If the fire didn't burn it, the water washed it away. There's really nothing left to salvage, but insurance should cover some of it."

"It's going to be all right," Rachel said. "We'll figure everything out."

"What are we going to do tonight, though? I mean, that was our home."

"I'd be more than happy to take you to a local motel for the night."

While Rachel wasn't happy with the situation, they didn't have any other choice. Their ride and home had both been wrapped into one, and now they were gone. The fire had taken everything from them. Still, they accepted the offer to get a ride. Neither of them liked staying at motels, but they were going to be together. Even though Becky had been shaken to the core, she had still managed to get her phone out and record the RV burning. Rachel couldn't blame her, but she knew they were going to have to come to some kind of agreement on what to do next.

She worried her sister would want to take a break, and she'd be stuck doing the one thing she wasn't ready to do—settle down. They both climbed into the back of the cruiser as she took another look in the direction of what was once their home. Rachel was still shaken to the core. First, the nightmare had woken her up, only to be living in a real nightmare of fire. She didn't understand what had happened, but she was still glad they had gotten out before anything worse could happen.

"You know, we're going to be all right. We'll figure out what to do next and just move on from there," Rachel said.

Becky didn't say a word. She was already online, posting the video of the fire and updating their fans as to what had happened. It was definitely something they didn't have in common. While they were suffering from the loss of almost everything they owned, Rachel didn't care what the people online had to say. She tried to talk to her sister a few more times on the drive, but Becky never replied. Rachel couldn't tell if she was completely ignoring her on purpose or if she was too involved in what was going on online to be concerned with anything else. She shrugged and looked out the cruiser window.

While the stars still brought her comfort, something now felt different in her life. She just couldn't put her finger on it. Rachel smiled to herself when she looked over and her sister was still pounding away at the keys on the keyboard. A lot of people could have seen what she was doing as a coldhearted response to the tragedy, but she knew better. Everyone had their own ways of coping with things, and that was Becky's way of handling her emotions. Any time her sister was feeling worried or stressed out about anything, she would dive into the online world and post her feelings there for the world to respond.

She cared about her fans as much as Becky did, but they weren't the center of her life. Rachel had her sister and work to put herself into. She would spend her time working harder and dive into the next mystery, but she wasn't sure if that was going to work this time. Her sister already wanted to take a break before the fire. Now, there was no telling what she would want to do, but they would have to decide together as a team.

Rachel tried to reach out to her sister one more time before they made it to the hotel, but she still didn't respond. She could tell Becky was still too shaken up to cope with the reality of what was happening, but she knew she'd be okay. In time, they both would be. A few minutes later, the officer was pulling the cruiser into a local motel.

The officer guided them to the front desk and explained the situation to the man behind the counter. The two girls were still in shock. Rachel was thankful for the officer and everything he was doing for them. Though she knew it was probably in the job description, she still felt like he was going above and beyond to help them in their time of need. It didn't take long for the clerk to type them into the system and get them a room.

After helping them to their motel room, the officer gave them his card and told them they could get hold of him at the precinct if either of them needed anything. It was still early morning, or late night, depending on how one would look at it. They both showered quickly to rinse off the smell of smoke and lay in their beds.

"You know what this means, right?" Becky said, speaking for the first time since they left.

"What's that, sis?"

"We're going to need to get an upgraded RV as soon as possible. The sooner we get another one, the sooner we can get back on the road again."

"We'll talk about it tomorrow. For now, we both need to try to get some sleep."

Becky smiled and rolled over. While she was glad her sister was thinking ahead, Rachel wasn't sure what the future held for either of them. She wanted nothing more than to get back on the road, but over the past hour or so, she was starting to wonder if the best thing for both of them would actually be to settle down somewhere.

Her thoughts had been mixed since they had escaped the fire. Even earlier in the night, Rachel was worried Becky wouldn't want to keep up the work. Now, she honestly was thinking about putting down roots somewhere and settling in. As the thoughts continued to swirl around in her mind, she started to doze off. On the one hand, she loved going from place to place and filming what they would find. On the other hand, maybe it was time to get off the road and start a real life. She wasn't sure what to do, as she fell asleep for the second time that night.

3

Rachel slept like a log the rest of the night. She had no dreams or nightmares, but she woke with a start as soon as she heard a pounding at the door. It wasn't just a normal knock that would lead her to believe it was someone from the motel staff. It was one of those knocks that someone could see on television when the police were ready to break down the door. She sat up quickly and noticed that the room was still mostly dark. She grabbed her phone to check on the time. Rachel was shocked to see that it was barely six in the morning.

Grumbling under her breath and wondering who would be knocking that early, she removed the blankets and got out of bed. She looked over at her sister and chuckled when she saw that Becky was still sound asleep, snoring. Her sister could sleep through an earthquake if they ever were in one. Rachel had always been amazed at what Becky could sleep through. She remembered a time when the two of them were between foster homes, and they stayed at an apartment in the city. It was a normal building like every other one around, but the one they were staying in was right next to the train tracks.

While she would wake up every time one would start to go by, her sister never once woke up. Rachel looked around at Becky's bed. There were notebooks scattered all across it, and her laptop was still open next to her pillow. Whatever her sister had been doing the rest of the night, she knew Becky had stayed up late. After what they had just experienced, it was her way of coping with it all. Before she could make her way to the door, the pounding started again. Cursing under her breath, Rachel stumbled to it and jerked open the door.

While she had no idea what to expect when she opened it, she was surprised to see the middle-aged man, in one of the nicest suits she had ever seen, standing in front of her. He looked out of place in the area of Alabama they were in. The man looked more like an agent for the stars in Hollywood. The man smiled at her as he adjusted his stance.

"Can I help you with something?" Rachel asked.

"I'm sorry to come by at such an early hour, but I am looking for either Rachel or Becky Groves. Are you either of those women? I was told I could find them at this motel."

Rachel was stunned to hear their names come out of the man's mouth. After all, there wasn't anyone other than the officer who should have known where they were, and it caused her to be leery of the man from the start. She gave him another look over, but it didn't look as though he had just thrown a suit on just to meet them. Still, she didn't like the idea of some strange man knocking on the door. No one should have known was theirs.

"May I ask who you are?"

The man smiled and nodded but didn't say a word. When he reached into his inner coat pocket, Rachel took a small step back. The world was full of people who did nothing more than look for ways to hurt others, and she wasn't taking any chances. She was relieved to see him pull out a business card and not a weapon. He slowly extended his hand and handed her the card.

"My name is James Young. I'm an attorney, and I represent your grandmother's estate."

Rachel scoffed. "I hate to tell you, but we don't have any family, let alone a grandmother who would require a pricy lawyer such as yourself."

James chuckled. "I'm fully aware that you and your sister both grew up in the system, but I assure you that you're who I'm looking for. It's a good thing I found you and your twin."

"What do you mean?"

"It's just that we were running out of time to locate one or both of you," James said.

"You mentioned some kind of estate?" Rachel asked.

"Yes. I represent your grandmother and the property she owns. There are a lot of things we need to go over, but there's a little time left for that."

Rachel had no idea who he thought they were, but in all the years they had been on their own, no one had ever come looking for them. She suddenly found herself curious about what the man really wanted. They didn't have much to offer, but they were popular enough that scammers would try to swindle money out of them from time to time.

"So, you know we grew up in the system, but anyone can find out that information. It's public record."

James grinned. "I'm not here to try to get anything from you. I have all I need. It is my job, however, to track you down and make sure you have all the facts that you've never had before. There's a lot about your family that you should hear about. You and your sister both need to hear about it."

"Like what? We really don't know anything about our family other than the little we know about our parents, and even that isn't much."

"Well, before we get into any of that, we need to go over the paperwork."

"Paperwork for what?" Rachel asked. "It's early, and we've had a long night. I swear, if this is some kind of scam—"

"It's not, but this will help you to understand a little more about what I'm doing here."

Rachel watched the man open his briefcase and pull out a large manilla envelope. He handed it to her, and she reluctantly accepted it. It looked like a normal envelope that anyone could mail out, but it was thick. She instantly knew whatever the man was selling was going to have a lot of information to go with it.

James smiled. "You're more than welcome to take that and look it all over. It will explain all the things you need to know right now."

"What is this all about?"

"It has information about your family and the estate your grandmother owned. You can read over the information in the envelope, and when you're done, you can ask me anything you want."

Rachel was still skeptical, but curiosity was already getting the better of her. She nodded but didn't take her eyes off the envelope. James quickly explained to her that he would be there all day, and then he walked away. Looking up for the first time in several moments, she watched him get into an expensive-looking black car. She was in awe of the car but still confused as to why the man was there. They didn't have a grandmother or anyone, for that matter. She slowly closed the door, all the while her eyes not leaving the envelope in her hands.

She slowly made her way through the room and over to her bed, which was on the far side. As soon as Rachel sat down on the mattress, she opened the envelope and started to pull out the large amount of paperwork nestled inside. The cover letter had both her and her sister's names at the top, which surprised her but not as much as what she read next.

A gasp escaped her lips when she read the first

line. It simply said they were sole heirs to their grandmother's estate. Neither of them remembered their parents, as they had passed away when they were born. They had spent the rest of their childhood being bounced around from one home to another until they became old enough to be on their own and they hit the road.

Rachel knew her mother's name was Amanda Groves, and judging by the name on the legal documents, Patricia Groves was her mother, their grandmother. As she continued reading through the paperwork, she couldn't believe what it said. Not only were they the sole heirs to their grandmother's estate, but its estimated worth was set at around thirty million dollars. She had to pinch herself to make sure she wasn't dreaming.

At first, the idea of having that kind of money meant they could each do whatever they wanted. She had only dreamed of having that kind of cash, and now it looked like it wasn't just a dream. Though, suddenly, she was interested in the rest of the family they knew nothing about. They would finally have the chance to learn about where they came from, but something didn't feel right about it all. There was a twisting feeling in her gut when she realized what they were about to get into, but it wasn't her choice alone.

4

Rachel sat on the edge of the bed for several minutes. Even though she knew she needed to wake up her sister and tell her what was happening, she was too stunned to move. All the possibilities kept running through her mind. After what could have been considered the worst night of their lives after the RV caught fire, they were being blessed with the money to do anything they ever could have imagined.

She quickly scanned through most of the other paperwork, but it was filled with more legal jargon than she could understand. It was impossible to get past the dollar amount that they were inheriting. Finally, after a little more time trying to read through the documents, she got up and approached her sister's bed. Rachel jumped on the bed and put her arm around Becky.

"Hey, sis. Time to wake up. I've got something to tell you."

Becky groaned. "Can't you just let me sleep?"

"No, there's too much to tell you."

"Fine, what is it?" she asked, sitting up in bed.

Rachel spent the next ten minutes telling her sister about the lawyer who had knocked on the door. She explained everything she understood from the documents and told her Patricia's name and what it meant for them. For a moment, her sister sat in silence, trying to understand everything she had been told.

Then Becky broke out in laughter. "You really think that someone is just going to leave us thirty million dollars? Come on, Rachel. Even as tired and out of it as I am, I know a scam when I hear it."

"I've been reading through it all, and it's real."

"No way that some long-lost relative is leaving us an inheritance like that. I mean, we've gone this long and no one has come looking for us."

"Here, read it for yourself, then. It's not a joke, and it's not some kind of scam. I thought the same thing until I read the paperwork, but it's all real."

Becky's face went pale as she realized Rachel wasn't joking around. She quickly threw the covers off herself and took the paperwork. Rachel watched her sister's face as she read. She could tell when she was getting to the good parts when her expression changed. There were details in the letter and documents about the twins that no one could have known.

"Did you read all of this?" Becky asked.

"I read what I could understand, but a lot of it is legal stuff I know nothing about."

"I just don't understand why, after all this time, we're just now being told anything about where we came from. Mom died giving birth to us, and God only knows where our father was. Now, we find out this?"

Rachel sighed. "I felt the same way when I read through that. It's hard to believe, but it's as real as you and me."

"Even the hospital didn't know what to do with us because there wasn't any family they knew about."

"I know. That's why we were put into foster care. Still, even without the money being in the picture, we have a chance to learn everything we never knew about before."

"I don't know. It's just been us for so long. I don't know if I really want to know anymore," Becky said.

"It's easy to feel that way, but I'd rather know about them."

"Maybe, but according to this letter, we're going to have to visit the estate. I think that's a good idea."

Rachel wasn't sure it was a good idea to go. While she was all for finding out about her past, she wasn't sure she wanted to go to the place her family had owned. They never had been there for them before. Why would it matter now? Still, she knew her sister would want to go the moment Becky pulled out her laptop and started typing away.

"What are you doing?"

"We're going to have to go to the estate. I already looked it up, and it's only about an hour from here."

"I don't know, Becky. I think we should start trying to figure out what we're going to do now that we don't have the RV."

Becky chuckled. "See, that's even more of a reason that we should go. We could stay there for a short time while we figure things out. Think of it like another one of our adventures. Besides, it's not like we have a whole lot going on right now."

"Well, we need to hold off on going too far right now. The insurance company is going to have to come to appraise the RV, and then we're going to have to wait for the insurance money."

"Like I said, the estate is only an hour from here. We'll be close enough that we can come back if they need anything. Hell, they can come to us since it's so close."

Rachel knew she was fighting a losing battle with her sister. She had always been the one to enjoy the adventure of things, while Rachel had been more of the hardworking of the two. Still, it was an easy decision to make since Becky wouldn't let it go until she agreed to go. Finally, she gave up and nodded.

"I'm telling you, sis. This is going to be good for both of us."

Rachel shrugged. "I guess I'll call the lawyer and see what we need to do to get this started."

Rachel pulled her phone out and started dialing the number from the man's business card. She was only then realizing how fancy the car was and remembered how well the lawyer had been dressed. It all made sense when she thought about the thirty million that they were set to inherit. After a few rings, James answered the phone.

"What can I do for you?"

"My sister and I would like to visit the estate and talk about the rest of the inheritance."

"Oh, that's wonderful news, indeed," James replied. "I hate to tell you, but I'm kind of tied up with another client at the moment."

"That's fine. Just give me a good time, and we'll get together then."

"Perfect. How about this afternoon? I'll make sure I've finished with all my other clients by then, and we can discuss the estate."

Rachel agreed and ended the call. Even with the excitement of the estate and learning about her past, she was tired. After the fire and getting to the motel late, she hadn't slept well. Having been woken up by the lawyer at such an early hour didn't help, either. She needed her rest, and she was already feeling the effects of the lack of it. Lying back in bed, she pulled out her phone and set the alarm. One way or another, she was going to get a few hours of shut-eye. She closed her eyes for a moment and was quickly interrupted by her sister's voice.

"That's the best idea you've had in a while." She smiled.

"I don't know about you, but I'm still exhausted,

and the lawyer can't meet with us until later anyway."

"If that's the case, then I'm going to get a few hours of sleep with you."

Rachel smiled and watched her sister climb back into bed. She reached up and clicked off the light. The thick curtains in the motel blocked out almost all of the light that shone through the windows. She was thankful for small favors and closed her eyes. After ten minutes of lying in bed, she knew she was going to struggle to sleep.

It was too much to absorb, even if she was exhausted. The idea that they were set to inherit millions of dollars was enough to keep anyone awake, but Rachel was thinking of the family she never knew. While they never knew their mother because she had died giving birth, her grandmother had been alive at the time. It was something she couldn't get over. They'd had relatives who were out there the whole time they were on their own.

Still, as she listened to her sister begin snoring again, she couldn't help but imagine what their lives would have been like if they had been taken in all those years ago. They never would have been put into the foster care system and had to practically raise themselves. Then again, she knew they wouldn't have become the women they were without the adversity they had faced as kids.

Rachel found herself thinking about the family once again. If their grandmother had the huge estate and the kind of money to leave the thirty million in inheritance, what else were they about to learn? The biggest question that rolled through her mind as she lay in bed, trying to sleep, was whether or not there were any other relatives out there that they didn't know about.

5

Rachel woke up to find herself in the middle of an empty field. The clear blue sky and the warmth of the sun beating down on her skin felt relaxing. She looked around to see nothing but wide-open space, along with the vibrant greens of the grass and trees surrounding her. It was like nothing she had ever seen before, and she raised her arms to the sky to soak it all in. The beauty only intensified as she heard the sound of fresh running water.

The sound was coming from somewhere off, not far from where she was standing, and she quickly rose to her feet and started to move toward the comforting noise. The closer Rachel got to where it was coming from, the faster it seemed as though the water was moving. She had always enjoyed everything nature had to offer, so it came as no surprise that she felt at peace.

It wasn't until she looked down at her feet and realized she was barefoot that she became confused. Why would she be out in the field without shoes? She didn't know the answer but kept moving toward the body of water. Nothing mattered to her at that moment, as something more than the rushing water called to her.

Suddenly, when the water came into view and she continued to move over the slope, everything became terrifying. Rachel quickly realized she was no longer in control of her body, though she tried to stop the forward progress several times. Something was pulling her closer to the rushing river.

Coming down over the slope, the river flowed wildly. The moment she saw that her body wasn't going to stop, she screamed. A panic rushed over her, but her body kept creeping forward. She tried to fight off whatever was in control, but nothing could stop her from walking directly into the water. Within moments, she could feel the undertow carrying her away. The water hit her with such force that it dragged her underneath and rushed into her lungs. She knew it was over. Her life light was slowly starting to fade as she drowned in the rushing water.

SUDDENLY, Rachel bolted upright in the motel room. The darkness of her surroundings frightened her for a moment until she remembered where she was. She gasped for air, struggling to catch her breath. The entire time she fought for air, she was screaming. It took several seconds for her to realize that Becky was right beside her, shaking her awake. Between the sound of her sister's voice and the constant ringing of the alarm she had set, Rachel pulled herself together.

It took her a moment to figure out that the entire thing had been a dream. It felt real to her. The water rushed over her body as she tried to fight the current, only to be pulled under. She could still feel the way it felt when the water pushed into her lungs, and she choked one more time.

"Are you okay?" Becky asked. "You must have been having one hell of a nightmare."

"I was, but I'm all right now. It was so real."

"I was worried about you for a minute. You've been freaking out for a couple of minutes, and I couldn't wake you up."

Rachel sighed. "It was just a dream."

'Well, I'm glad you're okay. It's just after ten now. Unless we want to pay for another night, checkout is at eleven."

'I guess we better get moving then."

Rachel could tell her sister was still shaken up about the dream, but there wasn't anything she could do to make her feel any better. It was the strangest thing, though, because she had never had a fear of water before, but now she'd had two dreams in a row she was drowning in. Still, she brushed the thoughts from her mind and packed up her things.

Becky was doing the same thing, and it didn't take long for them to get ready to leave. Rachel had made the two of them a cup of coffee, and they spent most of the next hour drinking their caffeine and talking. They were checked out of the motel before eleven, and they were waiting for their taxi to pick them up to take them to the local car rental location.

"What kind of car are we getting?" Becky asked.

"Whatever they have to offer. I'm not going to be picky."

"Don't be a prude, though, okay? I don't want a station wagon or minivan; they make me feel old."

Rachel laughed. "That's what you're worried about? We've been driving around a twenty-five-year-old RV for years, and now you're afraid of a van?"

"I'm just saying. Do you want to drive around looking like a 90s mom?"

They laughed, though her sister was right. She'd have to make a good choice of rentals when they got there. Before long, their ride appeared, and the two were headed to their next destination. Rachel had nearly forgotten about the nightmare by then. It was another thing her sister was good at doing. She had a way of making her forget all their problems. Her free spirit seemed to make light of the worst scenarios. Rachel wasn't sure if it was a gift or a curse. Either way, she was happy to forget.

By the time they made it to the rental place, they both were in high spirits. There was no telling what else the day would bring, but Rachel was looking forward to it. She had forced the strange dream from her mind—refusing to give it any more space in the already-crowded room. Thankfully, given their savings and bank statements, they finished at the rental dealership in a matter of minutes and were quickly back out on the road.

The clear sky and beautiful day were a welcome gift as they drove. The old rock music they listened to as kids was blaring on the radio, and Rachel was happy to sing along with her sister to every song they knew. Neither of them was in tune, but it didn't matter. Nothing was going to ruin the day they were having.

The estate was an hour south of them, and Rachel drove the speed limit. While both were excited to learn about the inheritance and property, they were enjoying themselves and not in any hurry. The warm weather made Rachel wish the rental place had offered a convertible, but she settled for having the windows down.

Suddenly, halfway through one of their favorite 80s ballads, Becky reached over and turned down the radio. Rachel tried to listen to the car, thinking she had heard something wrong with it, but she didn't hear anything.

"What did you turn the radio down for?" Rachel asked.

"I've been thinking about something, and I want to know your answer."

"Okay. Well, what is it?"

"Do you think there's more family out there that we don't know about?"

"I mean, we have no idea who was left out there or how much family we had to start with. Mom was our only link to any of them, but she was gone before we could ask. So, I have to think that there probably is a family member that we'll find out about."

Becky smiled. "I have to admit that I like the idea of having more family. It's always just been you and me, and I've loved it. I've just wondered what it would have been like having a large family."

"I've thought it before, too, but not since we were kids. Now, I don't know what I hope we find."

"Remember the stories we used to tell each other when we were kids around the holidays?"

Rachel grinned. "Oh, my God. I almost forgot about those. We always pretended to have a huge family reunion to go to, but our car would always break down."

"Neither of us knew what it was like to have a big family. So, we never wanted to make it there, but the thought was nice."

She smiled at the thought of how much fun they had as kids. It was always just the two of them, even when they had a foster family. Still, the excitement of what was coming crept in with every inch closer they got to the estate. When she realized they were only a few miles from getting there, Rachel's heart started to race. For the first time since they had started driving, she couldn't believe it was really happening.

Suddenly, she felt a churning in her gut. There was a fear she had never felt before growing inside of her. Rachel didn't know what they were heading into, but they were going to find out together.

6

Rachel was still going through the emotions of realizing how close they were to finding out more about their past as they pulled up to the address they were given by the estate lawyer. The moment the estate came into view, both sisters were blown away.

When most people think about the swamps in Alabama, they probably think about alligators and football. What stood in front of them was much more than that, and Rachel was in awe of the beauty. There were fields of weeping willows blowing in the light wind. They bounced in a way that seemed to mesmerize her. The house was something out of a storybook, and she couldn't take her eyes off it.

It was what you would expect from an old Southern house, but seeing it in real life was nearly more than she could take. She always had an eye for things that were old and beautiful, but this was the first time seeing an old Southern home in person, and she was stunned by its beauty. Giant pillars lined the driveway and the front of the house. The darkest of lush green covered the land as far as she could see.

Rachel brought the car to a stop at the end of the driveway and looked at her sister. Becky was just as amazed as she was, and they both got out of the car to marvel at the gorgeous estate standing in front of them. They were shocked as they looked at each other. A moment later, a woman who couldn't be more than a little younger than the two of them, along with a woman who looked to be in her sixties, approached them.

Without stopping to greet them, the older woman walked right up to them and wrapped them both in her arms. It was an awkward embrace, though the warmth and love in her hug didn't go unnoticed. "My name is Jessica Frank. Patricia Groves and I were friends for the longest time," she said, with a Southern accent. "We were probably best friends, if I'm being honest. This is my daughter, Grace."

"Well, I'm Rachel, and this is my twin sister, Becky. It's nice to meet you."

"With Patricia falling ill the way she did, my daughter and I took it upon ourselves to help her out. Before long, she just invited us to live with her, and we've been here ever since."

"Was she sick with something in particular?" Becky asked.

"Oh, it was just the old age getting to her. As we get older, our immune system doesn't kick it like it should. She was a wonderful woman. Patricia always said that we took care of her, but I'd like to think that she was taking care of us, as well."

"So, how long have you lived in the house?"

"Going on three years now. That's about the time she started to get sick," Jessica said. "We don't have to stand out here. Why don't you girls come on in?"

Rachel nodded, and the two followed Jessica into the house. They were amazed by the outside, but when they walked into the sitting room, it put the outside to shame. The lavish room was decorated in an old rustic and gold color. The maroon paint seemed to blend right in with the bright-gold trim covering the entirety of the room. She wasn't sure if it was real or not, but she had once heard stories of how people would trim their entire house in it.

"I have to say that it came as quite a shock when we were told about the two of you."

"Well, it came as quite a shock to us as well," Rachel said. "We didn't grow up with any family after our mother died, and we didn't even know we had a grandma."

"That makes a little bit of sense, actually. Patricia never mentioned having any granddaughters. She really never talked about her own daughter, Amanda."

"I didn't know if you'd even know her name. When we were born, Mom passed away. We didn't know anything about this or Patricia."

"Did you know our mother?" Becky asked.

Jessica sighed. "I'm sorry, dear. I never knew your

mother, either. Just had a few conversations with Patricia when she actually mentioned Amanda's name. I wish I could tell you more about her, but I didn't even move to the area until long after she had passed."

Rachel could tell her sister was disheartened. What little bit they did know about their mother could never have prepared them for what they had just walked into. She knew they would still have time to learn more about their family as they talked to the people around Patricia. Her mind was already starting to plan ahead as they looked around the massive room.

The old Southern home, from the outside, looked like any other Southern home built around the same time. You could tell there was more wealth to the owners than in other places, but the same, nonetheless. As she eyed the paintings on the wall and the massive chandelier hanging from the ceiling, she couldn't help but wonder what kind of woman their grandmother had been.

Still, the light conversation her sister was having with Jessica was keeping her busy, and Rachel was able to soak it all in. Even though she wanted to learn all she could about the history of her family, she knew there would be plenty of time to do so. She suddenly found herself grateful that Becky had talked her into coming, though something just felt off to her.

A single painting above the fireplace stood out, and she couldn't take her eyes off it as she moved in closer to get a better look. There was nothing unusual about the artwork, but the detail someone had put into it was perfect. She never understood the idea of someone painting a picture of a house just to hang it in the same house, but the time and effort spent on getting every detail right stood out to her.

"Any idea who painted this?" Rachel asked.

"I'm sorry, I don't know. Patricia never mentioned who it was done by, but there were entire days she would spend staring at it," Jessica said.

"It's really well done."

"Oh, she always said the same thing. I think I did ask her once why she had it in here and not in the family room, but she never responded. She'd just stare at it for hours."

Rachel understood at least part of the reason. Every stroke had been perfectly placed. Suddenly, there was a quick knock at the door, and Rachel jumped. Jessica immediately made a move toward the front door, and they all followed her. Though the knock had startled her at first, she figured it was just the attorney coming to finish the paperwork and explain the inheritance.

As they made their way back to the door, Jessica continued to point out little things and talk about their grandmother with joy and love. She could tell the woman had been close to her. It almost seemed like she was talking to her in a few instances, but friends who are close start to do that, eventually. Once people spend so much time together, they pick up on each other's quips.

Every room they walked through seemed to be just as lavish as the one before it, and Rachel was totally blown away. She couldn't believe how nice and perfectly decorated everything was. It was easy to see that a lot of time had gone into picking the right pieces for each room, and she imagined her grandmother had done most of that work. The woman had great taste.

Even though the place seemed to be perfect, there was something creeping her out. Rachel wasn't sure what it was about the house that made her shiver, but there was something. She quickly brushed off the thought. No matter how it made her feel, it was a beautiful home. Finally, they reached the front door just as another knock came.

"There will be plenty of time to talk about everything later. I hope we get to spend a lot of time together," Jessica said. "I'm really happy they found you and even happier to see you here."

"I hope so, too," Becky said. "This place is crazy gorgeous."

Jessica reached for the door and pulled it open. While Rachel looked up, expecting to see the attorney she had met that morning, that wasn't who was standing at the door. In his place stood a woman around Jessica's age. She stood there for a moment until she noticed an immediate tension that built in the air. She suddenly felt uncomfortable.

7

The woman glared at Jessica for a moment before pushing by her and Grace. Rachel had no idea what was going on, but she wasn't impressed with the way the woman acted from the start. Before she knew what was happening, the woman was standing directly in front of her with a smile on her face. She extended her hand, and out of respect for the house, she took it.

"It's so nice to meet Patricia's grandkids. She was my best friend for as long as I can remember. As a matter of fact, I'm her oldest friend. My name is Mary West."

Grace snorted, and Rachel caught herself looking around the woman and at the girl slightly younger than herself. She could tell that there was no love between the two, and she already had it in her mind to find out why.

"Y'all haven't spoken to each other in years," Grace mumbled. "Ever since that falling out."

If Rachel could hear the girl, then she knew Mary could as well. She hid the disdain on her face well, but she could see it was there. Instead of replying to Grace, Mary ignored her and kept a smile on her face. There was a story there that she wanted to know, but for now, there were other things to worry about.

Jessica reluctantly led the group back to the sitting room. She couldn't be sure about anything other than the fact that the three didn't get along, but she had no idea why. She found herself wondering what falling out Grace had mentioned. As they all headed back to the room, she couldn't get it out of her mind. Rachel tried to push the thoughts out of her head, knowing it wouldn't do her any good to dwell on something that was none of her business. She just hoped the attorney would be there soon so they could get out of the situation they were in.

"I always told your grandmother I'd be there for the two of you if something happened to her. She spoke very highly of you," Mary said.

Rachel didn't know what to say. Up until that moment, no one had known they existed. What made it even worse at that moment was that if Patricia had known about them, why hadn't she come to get them? Growing up in the foster care system wasn't for everyone. Even as she thought back to their past, she knew it really wasn't designed for anyone. They never had luck with any home they were placed in, and the entire time their grandmother could have come for them.

Rachel was suddenly overcome with anxiety. There must have been a thousand questions rolling through her mind for the woman. She tried to narrow down the ones that meant the most. If she could only get her mind to focus on one important question to ask, she could spit it out, but she was dumbstruck. Before they had a chance to continue the conversation, they heard a noise coming down the hallway. Rachel was happy to see the man in the expensive suit walking into the room. Suddenly, the pressure she was feeling was gone.

She watched James stroll across the room and join them in the arranged seats. As he greeted each person in the room, he seemed happy to see Mary there with them. He still had a smile on his face as he started to get himself organized. He pulled his briefcase from his side and placed it on the table next to him. He was soon pulling out documents and arranging them how he saw fit, and Rachel took a quick look around the room.

She spotted Grace first since she was sitting closest to her. The girl was lost on her phone, and she found herself glad that she didn't need her phone attached to her hip at all times. Even the slight age difference between them created a gap in technological advancement. Grace needed her phone to pass the time, and Rachel could enjoy the moment and view.

Her eyes continued to scan the room, falling on the two older women. Mary and Jessica were both glaring at each other, neither giving an inch to the other. She nearly busted out laughing at the looks they were giving one another. They were comical in the way that she had no idea what was wrong with the two of them. Still, curiosity was starting to get to her, and she knew she'd have to ask, eventually. When Rachel turned her head and looked at her sister, she smiled when she found Becky looking just as amused as she was.

"All right, I think I have everything all set," James said. "Are you all ready to get this out of the way?"

Rachel nodded and looked around the room, noticing everyone else was nodding as well. James pulled out a leather folder tucked in the back of his briefcase and slid out a single document. Though she wasn't sure what was written on it, she could tell it was an important one. Automatically, she assumed it was her grandmother's will, and that was why everyone had gotten there about the same time.

"This is Patricia's last will and testament. Patricia Groves, also known as the heir to the Groves estate, has given me the power to read this and delegate the following," James said. "The twins, Rachel and Becky, are heirs to almost everything that Patricia owned."

Rachel knew the reading was coming, but hearing it out loud made it all feel that much more real. She couldn't believe what was said. She and her sister were about to become the heir to everything that she had found herself awestruck by. As she looked around at everyone's faces, she fell on Becky's. Her sister looked like she was in shock. Quickly pulling herself out of her thoughts, she tried to focus on what James was reading from the will.

"Furthermore, the land, property holdings, and cash that she had in accounts and on hand are worth just a little over thirty million dollars. It now belongs to the two of you. There is, however, a small amount that has been set aside for an inheritance that will be left to Jessica and Grace."

"That can't be right," Becky said. "There's something wrong about all of this."

"I can only tell you what your grandmother's wishes were. I was there when she had this written, and I assure you this is what she wanted."

"It doesn't make any sense that she would leave us everything."

"Why doesn't it?" James asked. "You're her flesh and blood, and she wanted to leave everything she had to the two of you. It's quite common for family to leave their loved ones—"

"Exactly," Becky said. "Loved ones. We weren't her loved ones. How could she have known enough about us to leave us everything she owned, but she never once reached out or took us in when we needed it? That's what doesn't make any sense to me."

"I wish I could answer that for you, but I can't right now. I only know what Patricia wanted me to do, and that was to make sure the estate went to you and your sister. Anything more than that, I don't know."

Rachel sighed. "I'm with my sister on this. I've

been thinking about it a lot since this morning, and I have to say that the whole thing is kind of strange. We didn't have anyone from our family to help raise us, and we had to grow up in a broken system. Where was she back then?"

"I don't have any of the answers you're looking for, but I know where you might be able to find some," James said. "There's a family archive at the crypt. It should have your family history, and it's possible the answers to the questions you have might be in there."

With everything involving spirits she had dealt with in her travels, Rachel was intrigued by the crypt. She knew there would be a lot of history she could dig through, and she was already looking forward to it. Suddenly, she had another reason to move forward with the paperwork.

She glanced down at the table beside her and saw the paperwork with the lawyer's signature already on it. She knew she was just a signature away from possibly learning everything she wanted to know, and she was ready. Rachel looked back at James and smiled.

"Just tell me where to sign," Rachel said. "Also, I'm going to need to know where this crypt is."

James chuckled. "Now, hold on a minute here. We're not completely done here. There are a few more things we need to go over before anything gets signed by either of you."

8

Rachel gave him a puzzled look, and he just smiled at her. She was already intrigued by everything the man had said up to that point, even though she knew the majority of what was coming. Still, he had her attention.

"What else could there be?"

"There is a clause in the will that could keep you from getting any of the inheritance," James said. "Patricia thought very highly of family history and heritage. She wanted to make sure that you girls understood how important that was as well. So, she made sure to add the clause to the will to ensure you did exactly that."

"I don't understand what you mean," Becky said. "I thought that once an inheritance was signed, it was given to the person it was left to."

"In a lot of cases, it is, but not when it came to your grandmother. She wanted to make sure both of you felt how she did about the estate and everything that goes with it."

"What's that mean for us?" Rachel asked. "I'm sure it means that we have to do something to get the inheritance, but what is it?"

"The will stipulates that both of you must reside at the estate for no less than six weeks before the bulk of the funds will be released. Now, I've been granted the right to send you twenty-five thousand each as soon as the paperwork is signed. It will be wired directly into each of your accounts, but the rest of the funds will be in probate until you've completed the required time to release it."

Immediately after he finished reading the stipulations, Rachel felt uneasy. She didn't want to stay in a place she had never known. Not only was it all new to the both of them, but it also still creeped her out in a way she couldn't explain. Normally, the old property wouldn't have any effect on her, but there was something that caused her to pause her thoughts on staying.

"What happens if we decide not to go through with it?" Rachel asked.

"You mean if you don't agree to stay at the estate for the six weeks?" James asked.

"Yeah. What if one of us or neither of us wants to stay here for that long? What happens to the inheritance then?"

"Well, if that were the case, the money would be transferred to the estate trustee. If either of you doesn't want to stay, then the same thing would happen. The will dictates that both of you have to stay for six weeks in order to get the inheritance."

"So, it goes into the hands of the trustee, but what happens to the estate and everything else after that?"

"We'd have to start trying to locate another blood relative to take over the estate. If that never happens, then we'll have to exhaust all the resources your grandmother left behind trying. Keep in mind that the money helps run the place, along with part of it paying for me to find the two of you."

"So, does that mean we would get nothing?" Becky asked.

"That's right. If one of you doesn't stay for the required time, then neither of you will get anything out of the inheritance," James said.

Becky rubbed her hands together. "All right. Well, I've heard everything I need to hear. Tell me where to sign."

"Hold on, sis. We need to talk about this before we sign anything. This is all a lot for us to take in," Rachel said, stopping her before she could sign.

"That's fine, but remember when I said that we were lucky to find you and that time was running out?"

"I remember. I wanted to ask you what you meant by that, but I totally forgot."

"Well, you had thirty days from the date of Patricia's death to sign the contract. After that, the will is void, and we have to search for another blood relative."

"So, how much time does that give us?" Becky asked.

"Your grandmother passed away twenty-eight days ago. You have two days to decide, so I wouldn't waste it if I were you."

Rachel looked over at her sister and could see how angry she was with her. Judging by how excited she was to sign the contract, Becky was looking forward to staying at the estate, but she still wasn't sure if it was the right thing to do. Granted, the money sounded good, but there was still a bad vibe she was getting from the house, and she had been getting it since they walked through the front door. She stood up and motioned for her sister to follow.

"I'm really sorry about any inconvenience this may cause, but we have to talk it over between us before we can give you an answer," Rachel said.

"That's fine. Can you get me an answer by tomorrow?" James asked. "That will still give me plenty of time to get the paperwork filed with the court."

"I promise you'll have your answer from us by tomorrow morning."

He nodded, and the two sisters walked toward the front door. Even while trying to process everything happening and knowing her sister was angry with her, Rachel couldn't help but soak in the beauty of the house once more. It really was a work of art on its own. They made their way through the front door and back to the car.

As they sat in the rental before Rachel started to

pull away, she looked around at the view again. It was like something from a movie, and the setting was the early 1900s. If someone had painted the view she saw before her, they could never give it the justice it deserved. Rachel backed the car out of the driveway and headed back toward the motel.

Her sister was sitting in the passenger seat, but she hadn't said a word since before leaving the house. Rachel knew it was only a matter of time before Becky exploded, and then there would be an argument. Still, she was happy they were taking a moment to at least look at all the possibilities before answering whether they would stay or not.

It wasn't a matter of having to stay at the estate for her. She knew most of the larger inheritances were clouded with stipulations to make sure certain things were done before just anyone was given that kind of money. The problem was that the property made her feel uneasy, and she wasn't sure she could stay at the estate, no matter how much money was on the line. Mentally, she couldn't be sure she could handle staying at a place like that for longer than a few hours at a time, but she was waiting to hear from her sister before she tried to push her own feelings onto Becky.

They were only a few minutes into the drive when Rachel could feel the tension rising. A moment later, she saw Becky reach for the radio and shut it off. She knew the time had come, and she took a deep breath.

"I just don't understand, Rachel. I mean, after everything we've been through and how hard we've worked to get this far, why wouldn't you want the money? It's life-changing, and you'd never have to worry about it again."

"It's not just about that."

"At the very least, our viewers are going to love it. On top of that, it's just a measly six weeks. You could sleep the entire time, and no one would know the difference," Becky said. "Give me one good reason we shouldn't do this. I've just given you thirty million reasons we should."

"Something doesn't feel right about being there. I can't put my finger on it, but I get a sick feeling in my gut."

Becky sighed. "Here we go with your gut feelings again. I don't get how that trumps the millions of dollars we'll get by staying for six weeks. Think about how much we could do with that kind of money."

Rachel knew her sister was right, and just listening to the way she talked about it, she knew Becky was excited about the money. She had to admit there was more she wanted to learn about the house and family that was supposed to be hers. It wasn't right to make her sister pay for something she was feeling in her gut, and she knew it. Before she could respond, Becky spoke again, her excitement pushing through everything.

"What about our great plans of seeing the world? This is our chance."

Rachel sighed. "Fine, we'll do this, but it's not going to be as easy for me as it's going to be for you."

"Thank you. I promise you; you're not going to regret this. We're going to have a blast while we're there. Just wait and see. I can't wait to tell our followers what a crazy thing we're doing next."

9

Rachel quickly pulled off the side of the road and turned around. If they had been in any city around the world, she would have been struck by several cars. They were lucky to be in the swamp lands of Alabama, and she spun the car around without a single car going by. She knew they had only made it a few miles down the road, and it didn't make any sense to make James and the others wait for an answer they already had.

"We're really going to do this?" Becky asked.

"It's what you want, right?"

"I do, but I want it to be something you want, too. Don't do it just for me."

"I'm doing it for both of us, okay? I know my gut is telling me something is wrong with the place, but that shouldn't stop us from staying somewhere for that amount of money. Besides, I really want to learn more about where we came from."

"As long as you're doing it for the right reasons, then I'm okay with it."

Rachel smiled. "If I was doing it for any other reason, I'd tell you."

Becky laughed and turned the radio back on. Even though they were just down the road from the estate, Rachel didn't complain. She loved the rock as much as her sister did, and she wanted to let her enjoy the excitement she was basking in.

A few minutes later, the twins were pulling back into the estate's driveway. Before Rachel brought the car to a stop, she could see Jessica and Grace on the porch bickering. She found it odd that the two were fighting, but then again, she never knew what a mother-and-daughter relationship really was. As soon as she brought the car to a stop, the two women quit arguing. Even though the back and forth had quit, it didn't look anything like the relationship had looked when they had met the two before.

Rachel put the car into park, and they both climbed out. The bickering women on the porch now both had smiles on their faces and were heading in their direction. She could only think of how her sister felt just a few minutes earlier when they weren't going to stay and how much her attitude had changed when Rachel changed her mind. She quickly brushed it off as a family dispute and smiled back. Whatever problems they were arguing over weren't her responsibility.

She looked up at the house and smiled. Though the creepy feeling was still there, it was a beautiful house. There were two floors with a partial attic at the top. The roof had obviously been replaced since the house was built, but it was done in the same style as it would have been all those years ago.

Something caught the corner of her eye, and she glanced at the attic window. For a moment, she thought she had seen something move. Being three stories in the air, she couldn't be sure that what she had seen was real. As she squinted her eyes to try to get a better look, she thought she saw it again. Suddenly, she could see the shape of a woman looking down on them. A shiver ran down her spine as the figure glared at her.

Her heart started to race, and before she knew what was happening, Jessica and Grace were coming their way. Rachel moved her gaze to the two women coming to meet them by the car. After a quick nod of recognition, she glanced back up at the window, but the figure was gone. Whoever was in the attic moved quicker than her vision.

Rachel's heart was still pounding by the time the women had made it to them. She suddenly found herself fascinated with whoever else was living in the house. Neither of the women had mentioned anyone else when they had spoken earlier.

"What are the two of you doing back here?" Grace asked. "We didn't expect to see you until tomorrow morning when you let us know what you decided. Is everything all right?"

Becky laughed. "Everything is perfect. Actually, we didn't need all the way until tomorrow to decide what we wanted to do. We talked about it in the car, and we both want to stay here the six weeks. We figured it would be just as easy to come right back and sign the contract instead of waiting until tomorrow to do it."

"That's great. We were starting to think you were going to say no, but I'm glad you're choosing to stay. It will be nice to have someone else in the house."

"I think it's going to be fun for all of us."

Rachel barely paid attention to the conversation her sister was having with Grace. She knew they were planning to stay, but she couldn't take her eyes off the attic window after seeing the woman glaring at her. She wouldn't normally have been so obsessed with something like that, but if they were going to be staying in the house for the next six weeks, she wanted to know everything she could about the people who were staying there as well.

"Who else lives here besides the two of you?" Rachel asked.

Grace chuckled. "That's it. Just me and my mother. Before that, it was Patricia and the two of us. There hasn't been anyone staying here for a long time before that."

"What about the people who take care of the property?"

"It's just the housekeeper and groundskeeper. They stop in once a week to take care of everything, and then they're gone again."

"So, no one else comes in or out?" Rachel asked.

Grace laughed. "No, that's it. I have to ask, though, why are you asking something like that?"

"Honestly, I was just curious about who all has access to the estate. If we're going to be staying here for six weeks, I just want to know who else will be around."

"Well, if you go into town and start hearing any stories, don't believe them."

"What do you mean?"

"Well, the locals like to joke around and tell all the visitors that the place is haunted. They're good at telling stories, but in all the time I've been staying here, I've never seen anything like that."

"So, they just make up that stuff to scare out-of-towners? That's kind of a crazy thing to do," Becky said.

"It's something to pass the time, I guess. That's all it is. Just a bunch of locals sitting around making fun of people who think that stuff is real."

"What about Jessica?" Rachel asked. "Has she ever mentioned seeing anything like that around here?"

Instantly, Grace's face changed. She became irritated with the questions. Rachel knew she was asking something that most people didn't like to talk about, but she found herself immersed in the idea of the estate being haunted. Besides that, it was kind of in her job description.

The woman shook her head. "I honestly couldn't tell you what my mom has seen or what she hasn't. You'd do better if you just asked her for yourself."

Rachel looked around and quickly realized the

older woman had somehow managed to make her way back into the house. She had been so involved in trying to figure out who she had seen in the window that she didn't even notice the woman walk inside. She took a deep breath and promised herself she would pay more attention to what was going on around her.

"I guess I'll do that. I just figured she'd have mentioned it to you," Rachel said.

"Nope, but we don't tell each other everything, either," Grace replied. "Come on in. Besides, I guess this place is going to be yours soon enough anyway. As soon as you sign the contract, anyway."

Becky laughed. "Don't worry. We'll hold off on the eviction notice for a while."

Grace chuckled and led them into the house. Even seeing everything for a third time didn't slow her reaction to the house. Rachel figured it would take a while before she wouldn't be surprised by the interior of the house. They made their way down the hallway and back into the sitting room, where they found Jessica and James seated.

James greeted the two of them warmly, and he was happy to see they had made their decision so quickly. As the twins took a seat across from the well-dressed lawyer, Rachel's eyes drifted over to Jessica, who was seated beside them. The woman had her arms crossed and had an expression on her face that Rachel couldn't quite read.

As James reached back into his briefcase and pulled out the file for them to sign, it suddenly struck Rachel that Jessica was upset they were there. The look she was getting wasn't friendly, and she couldn't figure out why. The only thing she knew for sure was that the woman was not happy with the situation unfolding in front of her.

10

After the twins each signed their spots on the will and contract, Rachel walked with James to the front door. So far, he was the only one she was entirely comfortable with, but that was because he had been very helpful. He didn't waste time and explained everything they needed to know. Out of the four people they had met so far, he was the only one who didn't seem to be hiding something.

"I'll make sure to get this all turned into the courts in the morning. As of now, you're on the clock. Your six weeks will start today."

"I can't thank you enough for everything you've done so far. I do have to ask, for my sister's sake, when will the twenty-five be in her account?" Rachel asked.

James smiled. "I'll make sure it's transferred over as soon as I get back to the office. I'll keep in touch with you as well to make sure everything is going as expected, and we'll get you copies of all the paperwork so you can have it on hand."

"Sounds perfect to me. I think my sister is more excited about all of this than I am, but I can't wait to start learning all I can about Patricia and the life she had."

"The woman was amazing; I can assure you of that."

Rachel thanked him again and watched him walk to his car before heading back to the sitting room. Before she could make it there, she glanced over at the staircase and noticed Jessica waiting for her with a smug look on her face. She was already tired of the unnecessary attitude she was getting from the woman, but she approached her anyway.

"Is there something you'd like to say?" Rachel asked.

"You and your sister can take the two guest rooms. They've already been prepared by the housekeeper in advance and should have everything you'll need for your stay."

"Thank you for that."

"Don't get too used to it. We're not going to be waiting on you hand and foot while you're here. I'm sure the two of you can take care of yourself."

Jessica quickly retreated to her room while Rachel went and told her sister where their rooms would be. She wasn't surprised to see Becky take the first guest room. It was the second to last door on the right as they walked down the hallway. The last door was the room Rachel was getting. Each of the rooms had private bathrooms and a sitting room. It was quite lavish for a guest room, and she quickly found herself wondering what kind of people had come and gone through the rooms.

The two rooms were nearly identical, although each one was decorated entirely differently. As the two were checking out their rooms, Jessica came down the hallway and called for them. Rachel rolled her eyes but put on a smile before greeting the woman kindly.

"These rooms are amazing," Becky said.

"As is the rest of the house, I assure you," Jessica replied. "You'll be staying in these rooms for the duration of your stay."

"You know, I'm sensing some concern in the tone of your voice," Rachel said. "You understand that we're not here to change anything for you and your daughter, right? I mean, just because we own the place doesn't mean we expect anything from either of you."

"It's not my place to concern myself with such things. That's entirely up to the attorneys and the court system to decide. Now, if you'll excuse me, I have things to tend to."

Rachel didn't understand what the woman's problem was. It wasn't like either of them was going to kick the women out, so they had nothing to worry about. Shrugging off whatever Jessica and Grace were arguing about earlier, she quickly went back to her room and got herself settled in. She had to admit that it was going to be nice sleeping in a real bed after the years she had spent sleeping in the RV.

After she got her room settled, Rachel rushed over to her sister's room to check on her. She smiled when she walked into the room and saw Becky with her camera out, bouncing all around the space. While she had hoped she would wait before telling the world what was happening, she couldn't help but be happy to see her sister enjoying herself. She quietly posted up against the doorway and watched the show.

Becky was moving from place to place and explaining to all their followers the ins and outs of what she was recording. It was funny to see her trying to explain things she had never even seen before. Suddenly, through the happiness she felt from watching Becky's recording, Rachel felt a twinge in her gut, and her mind went to the woman who had shown her disdain for their very presence.

She quickly grew concerned with staying in the same house with two women who were so bitter and angry. Though Grace seemed to be more occupied with herself than anyone else, Jessica acted as though their very presence was ruining her life. She didn't know how to feel about it, but she understood they were going to be in for a long six weeks. Finally, her sister finished filming and looked over at her.

"Isn't this great?" Becky asked. "I told you it was going to be amazing."

"Yes, you did, and you were right."

"Did you ever think we would have our own rooms?"

"Not in a million years," Rachel said. "Did you see that we each have our own bathroom?"

"I did, and I couldn't be happier about it."

"Well, I'm going to go for a walk. Would you like to go with me and check out the place?"

Becky quickly nodded and grabbed her phone. A moment later, they were heading for the door, but her sister stopped and turned. Rachel could almost imagine what she was going to say before she said it.

"Why don't we see if Grace wants to tag along? I think we're going to get along with her."

"Maybe next time we can ask her. For now, I want to explore the property with just the two of us. After all, she knows all about this place, and we just got here."

Becky sighed and crossed her arms. "You're just not going to open up to anyone, are you? We're going to be living with these people for weeks. The least you can do is try to get to know them."

"It's not about getting to know them. It's about trust. We don't know these people at all. Even if they do come across as nice, we don't know who they really are," Rachel said. "I just want to get to know them before I go putting too much trust in the wrong people."

"You know how you get to know people, right?"

"I know I have to spend time with them, but I'm fine with it just being me and you the first day."

Rachel smiled. "I'm sorry I feel that way, but I promise I'll try."

"I know you will, and there is nothing to be sorry about. I'm actually glad you're cautious for both of us."

The two of them rushed down the front steps toward the main door. Rachel was anxious to get a closer look at the property, but Becky was the first one to reach the door. She chased her sister out the door and started to close it behind her. Suddenly, she froze in her tracks. There was something—or someone—watching them. The feeling had hit her like a ton of bricks, and it kept her from taking another step.

There was a slight breeze, but the sound she heard next sent a shiver down her spine. She could swear she heard someone whispering her name, but when she looked around, there wasn't anyone near enough to her to whisper. Her heart started to pound, and the sound took over every noise around her. It was then that she understood that it wasn't just a feeling she was having in her gut.

"Rachel? What are you doing? I thought you wanted to go for a walk," Becky said.

Rachel shook her head. "Yeah, I do. I'm coming. Don't worry about me."

She forced a smile and closed the door behind her. Rachel shook the disturbing feeling away from her and followed her sister. She knew it was probably just nerves getting to her, and she didn't want to upset Becky by telling her another one of her intuitions. Nothing was going to change the way she felt, and she needed to figure out what was wrong with Jessica. She thought she could just explain to her that she had no intention of changing things, but that had failed. She pushed the thought out of her mind and chased down her sister.

11

The twins were out to explore the property, and Rachel was excited to see what else the estate had to offer. She had seen the house from the front and most of the inside, but this was the first chance she was going to get to see anything more. There was a pep in each of their steps as they made their way around the front of the house. She could tell her sister was excited and even more so when Becky looked back at her and smiled.

"You know, James was telling me all about the estate."

"I saw the two of you talking earlier, and I read a little bit of what was here from the will," Rachel said.

"Well, the estate is roughly twenty acres with several other buildings on the property," Becky said. "James said that everything within the property line is ours."

"I recall seeing that in the paperwork, but I didn't

realize it was twenty acres. That's a lot of land to cover."

Becky laughed. "We don't have to explore it all in one day. We have six weeks to check out everything on the estate."

"I know, but it's crazy to think that all this beautiful property is ours. I never imagined we would own something like this. I mean, I figured we would find something a little smaller and off the grid, but this is amazing."

"Did you know, according to the documents, there are also another three properties as part of the trust? They aren't attached to this property, but they are somewhere in the area."

As they continued to walk, Rachel couldn't believe how stunning the landscape was. The wild marsh and trees perfectly blended in with each other, sending a blissful feeling through her. She could see her and her sister settling down in a place like that, but there was something that still wasn't sitting right with her. No matter how much she tried to push the feeling away, it came right back.

They had been walking for a while when Rachel thought she saw something off to their left. She wasn't much of a photographer, but the beauty the property had to offer made her think about getting into the profession. Someone with the right touch could make a good living taking pictures of everything they were seeing.

"You know, maybe we should buy a camera and

take pictures of what we're seeing out here," Rachel said.

Becky smiled. "I was thinking about the same thing. We could take the pictures and then load them up on the site to share with our followers. I think they would go nuts over a place like this."

"I'm glad we're thinking along the same lines. It's not like we're going to need the money, but I'd still like to keep the site going."

"We definitely don't need the money anymore." Becky laughed. "I always dreamed we would have a record-breaking video that got uploaded on the web, but this is even better. We didn't have to do anything to become millionaires."

The two sisters continued walking and talking. It was the first time in a long while that they were able to just relax and enjoy each other's company. Most of the time, when they were on a gorgeous property, they'd have to figure out how to make the most of their visit. Now, they had all the time they needed to explore. It was quite refreshing for Rachel, who loved spending time with her sister without feeling like they needed to complete a project for their fans.

They could see the edge of the swamp as they came upon a large limestone building. The worn path they were on led right to the front of it, and Rachel started to get a strange feeling in her gut. While Becky never believed in her feelings, she knew there was something to them.

Step by step, they moved closer to the old building. No matter how hard she tried to push away her feelings, Rachel couldn't shake the thought that they were being watched. She had looked around the area several times, but each time she'd glanced to the left or right, there wasn't anyone there. Still, they approached the old limestone building and made their way toward the small cemetery surrounding a large crypt.

Rachel knew this was the spot that James had talked about, and her heart started to race as she thought about the names they were about to see. The family crypt was a place where she could learn about their history and where they had come from. It was something she always wanted but had no idea how to find out without any family history.

The building itself was the size of a double-car garage. Not one of those small ones that attached to the side of a house, but the full-sized kind that stood alone. There were a few dozen headstones around it, with an iron fence wrapping around it all. It looked like something out of a creepy movie, which was fine with Rachel. She loved the scenes filmed in the oldest of cemeteries.

"This is actually quite gorgeous," Rachel said. "I mean, in a creepy kind of way."

Becky scoffed. "You and I have completely different versions of what beauty is. I can tell you that."

"Come on. You don't think there is something about the limestone building that brings out my eyes?"

"Maybe, if you are part of the living dead."

"Hey, don't joke about the living dead while we're walking through a cemetery. Besides, zombie movies are pretty awesome if you think about it. Actually, maybe we could get some director to film a movie right out of here. With the right lighting, I think they could really make something work."

Becky laughed at her, but she could tell her sister was thinking about it. It wasn't something Rachel had ever thought of before, but as she looked around the area, it made the perfect location for some kind of apocalypse film. The twins continued to joke around and tease each other as they made their way through the headstones, reading the names on each one.

Some of them dated back hundreds of years, but they all had the same last name as the sisters. Rachel marveled at the names of family members she never knew about. Each of them was some distant relative they could only read about now that they were gone.

"I wonder who these people were when they were alive," Rachel said.

"You know, we could always go into the crypt and see what kind of information is in there. Isn't that where James said we could find it?"

"That's right. He said the answers we were looking for might be in the crypt."

She remembered the conversation with James as soon as she laid eyes on the crypt, but it never hurt to let her sister think that she remembered something before her. Though they were the same age, Rachel always felt like the older sister who needed to look after the younger one, even if Becky was only a few minutes younger. They both rushed to the door, but they quickly realized it was locked.

Rachel was disappointed that they would have to wait to get inside. From the moment they had found out about it, she wanted to know everything she could about Patricia and the family she never knew. She sighed out loud and looked over at her sister.

"Say, why don't we go back to the house and explore there? Maybe we can find a key," Becky said. "If not, then we can just ask Jessica about it. I'm sure she knows how to get into the place."

"I don't know. Jessica hasn't been the most helpful person in the house."

"Yeah, probably not. Still, I think it's worth a shot. I want to know what's in there as much as you do, but we're going to have to get ahold of the key before we can do that."

Rachel sighed. "I guess you're right. I do want to go into the crypt, and Jessica is probably the only person who knows anything about a key to get in."

"Great," Becky cheered. "We can get the key and come back later to open the crypt. If it makes you feel better, we can go down to the small village and take a peek around there, too. I'm anxious to find out what kind of ghost stories the locals really talk about."

She smiled, but deep inside, she knew something was wrong with the property. They started their return to the main house, but Rachel kept thinking about the way she had felt since they had arrived and how there was a constant feeling of being watched. Something strange was going on at Red River, but there was no chance that anyone was going to believe her.

12

Though she was still disappointed to find the crypt locked, Rachel was excited to talk to Jessica about getting the key. She knew the woman had something against them, but she had to know somewhere inside herself that the twins didn't mean to come into their lives and change anything. Eventually, she knew the two would have to have a conversation about what was going on between them.

As the two walked in the front door of the house, Rachel's breath was taken away. She wasn't sure that she'd ever get over how well-decorated and lavish the place was. Each of the rooms had its own bathrooms, though some were smaller than others. They hadn't gotten the opportunity to see the entire place yet, but that was fine with her. It wasn't her place to go snooping in the other two women's bedrooms.

Rachel and her sister started going room to

room, checking out everything each area had to offer. After a quick look through most of the spaces, they had counted nine bathrooms in total. It was something that surprised her, even with how big the place was. Most houses, even the mansions, had half bathrooms, but every single one they had seen was a full bath. The five bedrooms looked mostly the same from what she could tell, aside from how they were colored and decorated.

The pair had made it through the majority of the house. From each bedroom to the informal dining room, sitting room, parlor, and study. They were making their way to the library—a room they knew would quickly become their favorite—when they were stopped by Jessica, who was standing at the doorway. Dread washed over Rachel even though she knew they didn't have a choice in speaking with her.

It wouldn't have been that bad with how Rachel had started to prepare herself for the conversation, but the woman said nothing as she stood in the way and glared at them both. She suddenly felt like a little child ready to be scolded. She instantly knew if the woman continued to give them grief over everything they did, things were going to come to a head. If it wasn't Rachel that ended up saying something, it would be her sister, Becky. Neither of them had the patience to deal with the attitude they were receiving.

"I demand that one of you tell me why you're

snooping around the house? Some of us enjoy our privacy," Jessica fumed.

Rachel scoffed and was instantly on edge. "Look, I know you don't like us being here and this is all a change for you and Grace, but we have every right to be here. Now, we've made sure not to go into anyone's room. We're just looking around the house."

"It doesn't matter how careful you are. We're the ones who have been living here for three years."

"I understand that, but after all, this is as much our house as it is yours. We're not planning on doing anything to jeopardize what you have, but we belong here, too."

"I wouldn't go getting too comfortable if I was either of you."

Rachel was full of rage. She had no idea what problem the woman saw in the two of them being there, but it was starting to get old rather quickly. As much as she wanted to rip into Jessica, she knew they were still guests in the woman's home. It was more Grace's and Jessica's than it was theirs, no matter what blood relation they had with Patricia. She quickly decided to bite her tongue. It wasn't worth getting into a full argument with the woman on their first day at the estate.

"We didn't mean any harm," Becky said. "We're just trying to explore as much of the estate as we can. We never knew about Patricia, but we'd like to know who our grandmother was and what she was like. James mentioned the crypt, but when we went out to look, it was locked. Do you have the key to the door?"

Jessica scoffed. "We lost that old key years ago. It wasn't something Patricia ever talked about, and I certainly never got the key from her."

Just by the way the woman said it, Rachel didn't believe her. Something about Jessica made her wonder how much she would be willing to lie about. Still, she tried to hold back her temper as the rage in her heart started to grow. They merely wanted to learn about the family, not take anything away from anyone else.

Rachel shrugged. "That's all right. I supposed we can call a locksmith and have him come out to open it."

"Maybe, but I bet we can find something lying around her to just cut it open with. Either way, we'll get in there somehow." Becky smiled. "Thank you, anyway."

Jessica just glared at them for a moment. It was easy to see the woman was debating something in her mind, but Rachel was in no hurry to pressure her anymore. She knew if they just gave her a few moments to think it through, she'd make the right decision. Finally, after several minutes of silence passed, Jessica sighed.

"I think there was a spare somewhere, but I'm sure it's going to take us a few days to find it."

"That's fine," Rachel said. "We have plenty of time, and there are a lot of other things we can find to do until then. The estate is massive, and we both want to see as much of it as possible."

"I don't think I ever remember seeing it, but maybe in passing, I heard Patricia talk about it. I'll see what I can do about finding it, but like I said, it's going to take a few days."

Rachel smiled. "We'll give you two days to find it, then we'll cut it off or call a locksmith."

Jessica shrugged and stormed by them, bumping into them both as she passed. She couldn't believe the woman's hateful glares. Neither one of them had given her a reason to be upset with them, but Rachel was starting to wonder what Jessica was hiding. No one would act that way for no reason unless they were trying to keep something a secret. She shrugged and nodded at Becky. They both started walking back through the house and to the front door.

"That was kind of awkward, don't you think?" Becky whispered.

"It was more than that. I swear the woman hates us, but I don't understand why."

"No clue. I guess she just got used to living in the house alone with no one other than Patricia and Grace around."

"Maybe, but now I'm worried about how far she will take it. If she hates us enough to be that rude on the first day, what else could she be capable of?"

"Great, now I'm worried about it, too," Becky said. "Do you think the doors on our bedrooms lock?

I would hate to wake up in the middle of the night to find her standing over my bed."

Rachel laughed. "God, can you imagine? Still, I don't want to think about that."

"Me either. Just six weeks, then we are out of here. We can travel to all the places we ever wanted, and we'll be in a new RV."

"With comfortable beds and air conditioning."

Becky chuckled. "The lifestyles of the rich and the famous."

The two walked out the door and straight to the car. Rachel was mostly happy with how the day had been going, despite the few run-ins she'd had with Jessica. Every time the two spoke, she knew the feeling was only going to get stronger. She was proud of how she had handled each situation so far, but things weren't going to last like that forever. There would come a breaking point, and Rachel knew it.

As she climbed into the passenger seat, she was excited to see what the town had to offer. Just when they both started to put on their seatbelts, each of their phones chimed at the same time. The twins gave each other a puzzled look and reached for their phones. Instantly, they both grinned at one another. The twenty-five thousand that James said would be deposited in their accounts had come through.

While she had no idea what she would use it on yet, it felt good to have that much in the bank at one time. Becky quickly put the car into gear, and they headed down the driveway. Even as carefree as she felt, there was a twitch in her gut again. Looking in the side mirror of the car, she glanced up at the attic window again. Rachel couldn't see anything this time, but something definitely was wrong with the house. Her stomach twisted at the thought, but the house was soon out of view.

13

It was nice to enjoy the view from the passenger seat. Since they had picked up the car from the rental dealer, Rachel had done all the driving. She was amazed at how much she had missed by having to pay attention to the road instead of the view. It was as beautiful on the ride to town as it had been driving to the estate. It was nice to see the little things that had been missed the first go around.

The few houses that lined the roads were nothing in comparison to the one they were staying at, but they had a charm of their own. The tall emerald grass was a regular theme throughout the area, and she didn't mind it one bit. When they finally reached the village they had been excited to see, it offered a view that she had only seen on television.

It wasn't as fancy as the New Orleans area they had visited before, but it definitely brought a local feeling of hospitality. The streets were lined with carts, and the buildings that filled the village were full of all sorts of shops. The twins quickly parked the car and hopped out.

"I can't wait to find a camera to take those pictures with. I really think our followers are going to dig what we have in store for them next," Rachel said.

"They're going to like it, that's for sure. I want to see how they react to the videos we post of the estate. I'm already excited about their reactions to the bedroom."

"How's the attention been on the site since you let them know about the estate? I haven't had the time to check on it."

Becky smiled. "About as good as you think it would be. Everyone has been sending us a ton of love and well-wishes. I'd venture to say that we have the most caring followers out there. It's truly amazing the things they are saying."

"I've known that since the day we started and only had one hundred people following us. What about new viewers?"

"You're not going to believe it, but we've had ten thousand people sign up to follow us since I posted about the estate. I can still hardly believe it."

Rachel couldn't believe it. They had been working on the site and building their list of followers for years, and it had still taken them that long to get to where they were. Now, in a matter of a day, they had grown nearly ten percent. It was truly an amazing feeling to know they were reaching so many people, and the outcry of support was still flooding in.

The twins were still standing by the car, looking at everything throughout the village. It was smaller than she had expected, but the town seemed to be bustling with people. Rachel was blown away by how full of life the small town was. The Southern charm stood out in all its glory. Still, it was easy to see that they were outsiders, as all the bystanders that walked by them continued to gawk until they were out of view. She didn't mind the attention as long as none of them looked at them the way Jessica had been.

Rachel shrugged and nodded to Becky. She was ready to see what the small shops had going on for them, and she was ready to find a camera to take photos of the estate. As they walked toward the closest shop with a window, people greeted them with the hospitality you would expect from the south. Nothing but smiling faces and friendly waves. She nearly felt as welcomed as she thought she would if they had a hometown to walk through.

Suddenly, Rachel heard a familiar voice coming from behind them. It wasn't the kind of voice she had heard much of, but she knew who it was before they turned around. She wasn't surprised to see Grace standing behind them, but what was surprising was the man standing next to her. He was quite handsome and had a charming smile. His dark black hair poked out from the bottom of his ball cap. He was slightly built but not bulky. She could tell he liked to keep himself in shape. He smiled at both of them, but his focus was on Becky.

It didn't take long to see the man had eyes for her sister, but she couldn't blame him. Even though the sisters were twins, Becky always had an eye for fashion. It's one of the reasons they worked so well together, besides the obvious family ties. For everything they had in common, there were always as many things they did differently.

Becky always wore her clothes a little on the tighter side, and she liked to keep things baggy and loose. From time to time, Rachel would wear makeup and go out, but that was an everyday occurrence for her sister. Between the two, Becky was more of the high-profile influencer people loved to look at.

"We didn't expect to run into you here," Becky said.

"Well, we're just out doing a little shopping of our own. I'd like you to meet Zach Ivory," Grace said, lacing her arm through his. "Zach, this here is Rachel and Becky Groves. They're the heirs to the Red River Estate."

They both smiled and said hello. It wasn't long before she could see that Becky was bored. While she always liked to flirt and hang around all the cute guys, her sister would shut down when she found out a guy was taken. Rachel smiled when her sister excused herself and dipped into the art and bookstore a few buildings over. For a moment, she wished she could do the same.

"Hey, I was thinking about something," Grace said.

"What's that?" Rachel asked.

"The two of you should join us for dinner tonight. It would be nice to have some company that isn't quite as boring as the regular crowd."

"I'd like to do that, but Jessica doesn't seem to be thrilled to have us there. Actually, I'd venture to say that she isn't happy about it at all."

Grace laughed. "Well, she's been going through a lot, but it's all right. She's going to be over at a friend's house tonight anyway. We'll have the house to ourselves, so you should join us. It will just be me, Zach, and the two of you. It will be fun. I promise."

"If that's the case, then we'll join you."

She could tell the couple looked excited about having company, but she was ready to get herself out of the awkward situation. Rachel promised they would be there for dinner, and she quickly made her way into the store she saw Becky run into. As she looked for her sister, she found herself glad to have the opportunity to talk to Grace without Jessica jumping down their throats.

Grace might be able to offer the twins some insight about Patricia Groves and the history of the house. She had to admit that she was hoping to get more answers about the house at that point, especially with the strange sensation that kept overwhelming her when she was there. Quickly finding her sister, she told her all about the plan to join Grace and Zach for dinner.

"Man, I can't wait," Becky said. "I'm so glad she's not like Jessica. I don't know how much more of that woman I can handle."

"You and me both. I just hope we can finally get some answers about the house and maybe learn some new things about Patricia."

"Well, Grace is going to be our best chance of doing that. It doesn't seem like her mother is going to be much help on that end of things."

Rachel laughed. "I don't think she's going to be willing to help us with anything."

"That's true, but I think I need to exit stage left."

"What?"

Becky nodded toward the front door, and she turned around to see what she was talking about. Rachel rolled her eyes when she noticed the handsome man walking through the entrance, giving Becky a wink before he stepped behind the counter. Without missing a beat, her sister sauntered over to the man.

Rachel knew her sister couldn't help herself. She was a flirt by nature, never missing the opportunity to talk to a good-looking guy. Rolling her eyes once again when she saw her twin lean up against the counter and start to talk to the man who had just walked in. She shrugged and quickly went back to browsing the shelves.

Her mind raced with excitement for dinner with Grace. They had been stonewalled at every turn when they tried to learn anything about their family history, but maybe it would be different this time.

Rachel pushed the thoughts from her mind and focused on the shelves in front of her. She didn't know what she was looking for, but there was time to find it as her sister flirted with the attractive stranger at the counter.

14

After what she considered a successful shopping trip to the village, they were on their way home with all their purchases. Rachel had found a camera that should suit the needs of what she was looking for. It had taken her a while to choose, but when she finally made her decision, it felt like the right one. The drive back to the estate was perfect, and the two of them blared the music for most of the trip. Both of them were happy with the time they had spent in the village, but Becky looked delighted for some reason. She reached over and turned down the radio.

"You're awfully happy for someone who spent more time talking to Grace's boyfriend than she did shopping," Rachel said.

Becky grinned. "Well, that's because they are no longer together."

"Really? It looked like they were getting pretty friendly when we ran into them."

"Yeah, that's because they're still friends. They actually broke up last month, but they wanted to stay close. From what Zach was telling me, they have a lot in common."

"I bet they do," Rachel sneered. "I bet they share a lot of things together."

Becky laughed. "Hey, you know I wouldn't flirt with a guy who was taken, but since he made the first move, I had to have a conversation with the man. I mean, you saw the guy."

"I know, but it was kind of weird overall, don't you think?"

"A lot of people break up and stay friends nowadays. Things are a lot different than they used to be. Besides, if you want to keep shopping there, you're going to see him quite frequently. He owns the shop."

"That might come in handy, actually." Rachel laughed.

"Discounts," Becky cheered.

"Not like we need them now."

"That was my thought, too. Zach told me he's owned the store for about five years. He came back to the area when his dad passed away from a heart attack."

"That's sad, but at least he can keep his father's memory alive by continuing to run the shop."

Becky smiled but looked to be off in her own thoughts. She turned the radio back up just as another one of their favorites came on. Whatever station they were listening to seemed to know exactly what kind of music to play. About twenty minutes later, they were pulling up to the house, and Rachel was happy to see Jessica's car was nowhere in sight. After the day they'd had with the woman, she didn't need another episode.

Though there wasn't any sight of Jessica's car, there was another car in the driveway that she recognized. She remembered it from earlier in the day when they all had gotten together to hear the will. Mary West's car was parked up by the house, and after a quick glance around the property, Rachel could see the woman sitting on the front stoop. She wasn't sure what the woman was there for, but she was hoping the conversation wouldn't end up like the ones they had with Jessica. The two were nearly the same age, and it was obvious they had problems with one another.

The woman started to wave at the twins the moment they made eye contact. Rachel was glad to see the woman seemed to be in high spirits, and she gave the woman a slight wave back. There was no harm in being nice to the people around them. At least until she knew what kind of people they really were.

As Rachel undid her seatbelt and started to get out of the car, she glanced up at the woman sitting on the stoop again. Mary was holding something in her hands that Rachel didn't recognize at first, but Rachel quickly saw what looked like a bag of dead flowers dangling from the woman's hand. At first, she didn't know where they had come from, but she quickly realized they were from the cemetery and that she had seen them during their visit earlier.

"What are you doing with the flowers?" Becky asked as they approached the woman.

Mary smiled. "Oh, these are the ones from last week. Ever since Patricia passed away, I have come every week to replace the flowers on her grave. We never said anything to each other, but I know my friend would have done the same thing for me."

"That's actually a really nice thing to do."

"I know I don't have to, but I also know it would make her happy to know someone was still looking over her."

Rachel smiled. "I thought I recognized them from the cemetery. Becky and I took a stroll around the property earlier today."

"It's a beautiful plot. Patricia never wanted to leave this place, and I can understand why." She chuckled. "I guess she never has to now."

"What was she like when she was alive?"

"She was a strong and smart woman. There wasn't anything she couldn't handle on her own. I think she would have liked to have met the two of you."

"Did our grandmother have many friends during her life?" Rachel asked.

"Your grandmother knew a lot of people, but I don't think she called very many of them friends. Still, we had each other for most of our lives. The estate has been around for a very long time, and Patricia was here for most of it."

"How long ago did the two of you become friends?"

Mary chuckled. "Longer than I'd like to admit. Still, I remember how wild Patricia and I were fifty years ago. We made a lot of fond memories together. From sneaking away after dark to drinking near the swamp. We both were quite the handful."

Rachel smiled as she thought about her grandmother running wild through the estate as a child. She didn't know much about the woman, but it sounded like she had lived a happy life while she was here. Suddenly, they heard a car pulling into the driveway, and she turned around to see that it was Grace's. Mary didn't waste a moment of time as she excused herself and headed for her own vehicle. Within a minute or two, the woman was pulling out of the estate and long out of sight.

Though the amount of tension between the two was nothing in comparison to what Rachel felt with Jessica, it was easy to see it was there. However, she was curious about what had happened between them that was causing such distance, but it wasn't her place to interfere with whatever was going on between Mary and Grace. The twins quickly followed their new friend into the house, and Rachel brushed off the tension.

"I hope you don't mind," Grace said. "But I need to lie down for a while. We're still on for dinner."

"Okay," Becky replied. "Is there anything you suggest we do until then?"

"If you haven't been to the library yet, it's full of

great books to read. That is, if you're into that kind of thing."

Rachel smiled. "I know I could use something good to read. Thank you."

Grace nodded and disappeared down the hallway. She wanted to make sure that the young woman was feeling all right, but before she could say anything, she was gone. She shrugged, and the twins headed in the opposite direction toward the library. Rachel was excited to see what kind of books were kept in the large library.

As soon as the two opened the library door and stepped in, she was blown away. It was decorated in the same way as the rest of the house, but each shelf was lined with its own gold trim, and the deep purple meshed well with the bright-gold plating. Rachel was quickly overtaken by the beauty of it all. They quickly split off in two directions and started to look around at the rest of the room.

Suddenly, Rachel was overwhelmed by the feeling that they were being watched, but it wasn't the same as before. This time, she had the strange sensation that someone was calling out for help, but it was directed toward the twins. She wouldn't have been able to explain it if she had tried, but it was a feeling she couldn't shake. A shiver ran down her spine like someone had run their finger down it. The cold sensation running through her body was hard to ignore, though she tried to anyway. Brushing off the feeling as best she could, she continued gazing at the quite large selection of books in front of her.

Rachel ran her fingers over the spines of several books. Many of them she had never heard of before, but there were some that she remembered fondly reading when she was younger. Out of nowhere, the tip of her finger ran across a book engraved with their last name. Intrigued by the writing, she reached for it.

15

*T*he moment her hand touched the binding of the book, she knew something was different about it. Rachel wasn't sure what she was thinking, but as soon as she tried the pull the book off the shelf, it didn't move. Tugging on it again, she expected something to happen, but it still didn't budge.

"Hey, Becky. Come check this out."

"What is it?"

"Just come here."

Becky scoffed but moved over to where she was standing. They both inspected the book after her sister tried to pull it out but had the same result. Neither of them could get the book to move. As they looked around to see what was keeping it on the shelf, Rachel could tell it wasn't a traditional book. It was covered in dust, like it hadn't been touched or cleaned in years. She would have expected that from an old house that wasn't lived in, but she quickly remembered Grace had mentioned a housekeeper. It should have been well-dusted by the time they had gotten there.

Still, the two started looking around for something that would keep the book in its place but didn't find anything until Becky reached up and found a lever on the back of the book. Surprised by the finding, she tugged on it, but nothing happened.

"What do you think it does?" Becky asked.

"I don't know, but a lot of these old houses have secret passages. I bet it used to have something like that, but it got closed off, and they forgot to remove the secret lever."

"Wouldn't it be cool if it had worked? We could have recorded what we found, and our followers would have gone nuts."

Rachel smiled. "You're right about that, but I don't think this one is going to do anything."

A second or two later, they started to hear the sound of gears moving behind the bookcase. She was shocked to hear the noise when they already thought that it wasn't going to work. Clearly, she had been wrong. Suddenly, the book started to move, and it quickly gave way. It tilted forward, but it didn't fall off the shelf. A large section of the shelf popped out. It was the size of a doorway, and Rachel couldn't believe it.

There weren't many things that she was right about when they went to new locations, but knowing they had just found some sort of secret passage made her grin. The twins looked at each other, neither knowing what to say at first. Instantly, they started to work together to get the hidden door open so they could see what was behind it. It took them several minutes and a lot of patience, but they finally opened it enough to see behind it.

Rachel was surprised to see what looked like a second room behind the hidden wall. It wasn't a very large room but big enough to fit a small office of some kind. She wasn't sure exactly what they were looking at since the room was still dark, but from what she could see of it, she could tell it had the makings of a little office. It was just as lavish as the rest of the house, but most of it was quite outdated. The moment they opened the false shelf, she could tell the room was covered in dust and cobwebs. Whatever it had been used for in the past, it had been a long time since anyone had been in it.

The two of them took a step closer, and each reached a different direction. Both of them were feeling along each wall, trying to find some kind of switch to turn on a light. Finally, Rachel felt along the wall and touched something that felt like a switch. Flipping it in the opposite direction of where it was sitting, a light illuminated the room for the first time.

She couldn't believe what she was seeing. As she had suspected, the office hadn't been touched in many years. Her mind trickled to the thoughts of the family she never knew. Maybe they would find something in the room that they could each have as an heirloom. Never having known their true family, it was something they never had the chance to have growing up. Knowing there could be lost information on the desk, that was the first place Rachel went.

There were still old papers scattered across the top of it. Each was covered with its own layer of dust. Though it was already stuffy in the room since it had been closed off for so long, she took a deep breath and tried to blow off some of the dirt that had built up. Immediately, she noticed documents on the right side, and they were addressed to Patricia. Rachel smiled as she slowly started to realize that the room had been her grandmother's at some point in the past. She found herself wondering how many hours the woman had sat right there where she was now.

Sitting down on the chair in front of her, she suddenly found herself feeling closer to her grandmother. It was a touching moment to find a piece of Patricia's history that had gone untouched. Rachel ran her fingers across the top of the desk and down over the handles of the drawers. Their grandmother had remarkable tastes. As she opened the top drawer and looked inside, she was happy to see an old leather binder with Patricia's initials etched on the front. She quickly realized the binder was actually an old journal, and she grew excited about the possibilities.

"What did you find over there?" Becky asked.

Rachel pulled out the journal and dusted it off. It hadn't been opened in a long time. As soon as she opened it to the first page, her heart began to ache.

Knowing that her sister was curious, too, she started to read the first entry out loud.

"*Today was the first day that I've decided to write my thoughts on paper. I used to journal when I was a child, but it seemed silly as I became an adult. Still, as I watch my beautiful daughter, Amanda, grow up in front of my own eyes, I know I want to try to capture every feeling I can with her. Many people have warned me that children grow up too fast. I'm finding that out for myself now.*

"*Today, for instance, Amanda was running carefree through the field. It reminded me of a time when I was young a wild, too. My friend and I used to run carelessly around the estate, and I hope my daughter has more sense than I did. Still, it makes me happy to think she will grow up here and have so many fond memories, just like I do. She's the best thing to happen to me, and I hope she grows up to know I loved her with all of my heart.*"

She found herself wiping a tear from her eye, and the twins sat in silence, reflecting on what they had just read. It felt good to even find some small details about their grandmother and mother. Even if they never knew her, they felt the happiness in the woman's writing. It was like sharing a memory with a woman they loved but never got the chance to meet. Suddenly, they heard a voice calling them from downstairs. Rachel knew it was Grace waking up from her nap.

Grabbing the journal off the desk, she quickly stuck it under her arm and closed the drawer to the desk. She wasn't sure how Becky felt about finding the small room, but she knew she didn't want anyone else to know about it. There had been so much time that passed since anyone had entered the office. Rachel felt like it should be something they kept to themselves.

"I'm not telling anyone about this," Rachel said. "Agreed?"

"Cross my heart and all that." Becky smiled. "We'll keep this just for us."

"Let's close it back up for now."

They both grabbed a part of the shelf and forced the door closed. Rachel was happy to know they were on the same page, though it would have been different had Jessica not acted so hateful toward them. Still, after closing the door, they quickly slipped out of the library and moved down the hallway.

A few minutes later, they found Grace and Zach waiting for them. The moment she laid eyes on the two, Rachel found herself wishing she could skip dinner and do nothing more than go to her room and read more of the journal. She knew she couldn't do that to her sister, but the thought crossed her mind. Even if it didn't matter how she felt about them, they needed to keep up appearances that they were at least trying to make things work.

16

The twins had met the pair at the bottom of the stairs. Everyone had smiles on their faces, though Rachel knew hers wasn't entirely out of joy. She wanted to ensure they were trying to make things work between them all, knowing they would be spending the next six weeks living in the same house. The journal kept calling to her, though, and she wanted to spend the rest of the night learning about her grandmother through the entries.

Not wanting to be the one who killed the party, she reluctantly followed the others into the dining room. When they entered the dining room, Rachel thought it was strange to see two women she didn't know setting up the meal. While the food smelled amazing, she was used to fending for herself. Rachel and Becky had done a lot of taking care of themselves while they were growing up, and sometimes the best meal they would get was whatever they threw into their noodle packs.

"What's with the help for dinner?" Becky asked.

"Oh, it's nothing, really. I just decided it would be better to hire someone to help with the meal," Grace replied.

"Growing up the way we did, we never had the chance to have anything served to us like this. The closest I've ever been to having my food brought to me is in a restaurant."

"Well, I think you're in for a treat. They'll be handling the prep work on the food and bringing us whatever we need."

"You know, you're going to have to get used to doing things for yourself again," Zach joked.

The man was grinning from ear to ear, but Grace fell silent. For a moment, no one at the table knew what to say, and the time started to become awkward. Rachel tried to let it all soak in. It was true that the woman wasn't going to be in money like this for the rest of her life. Now that the twins were there, the bulk of the funds were going to transfer over to them. Still, it wasn't something she was ever going to throw in anyone's face.

"Do you have any plans now that everything is going to be changing?" Rachel asked. "I mean, nothing is going to be the same as it was when Patricia was here."

Grace sighed. "Honestly, I haven't thought that much about it. I figured with all the time I spent helping Patricia when she got sick, I was going to get something in the will. I had no idea I wasn't being left anything. I'm not mad. For the record, it's just unexpected."

It was a surprise to hear that Grace had been left out of the inner circle of the will. The twins didn't know anything about Patricia before the visit from James, and she still knew what was being separated out and to whom. Still, she had to wonder why her grandmother had left the young woman empty-handed.

"That's kind of strange because when James was reading everything off, it seemed like Jessica knew about the will and everything in it."

"Yeah, and that's exactly what we were arguing about on the porch when you guys came back. She happened to know all the details but never thought to say anything to me. I would have come up with my own plan had I known this was going to happen."

It made sense that the mother and daughter would argue over something like that. If she was in her shoes and Becky had done what her mother had done, she would have been angry, too. Still, after seeing how the woman had handled things, Rachel knew they would have to do something to make it right. Grace was nothing like her mother, and though she thought she would be included in the will, she wasn't expecting the money.

"Well, I wouldn't worry too much about that, Grace," Becky said. "We're going to make sure you're taken care of. You did a lot of good for our grandmother while she was alive, and you're a good person, too. I can tell by how you talk about everything."

"My sister is right. As far as we can tell, you can't be blamed for any of this mess."

"Seriously?" Grace said, trying not to get emotional. "You guys don't have to do anything. You know that, right?"

"It's not about what we have to do. It's about doing what's right. You shouldn't have been cut out of the will like that, especially after all that you've done. We're going to make sure you're taken care of the way you should have been," Rachel said.

"Thank you so much. I really don't know what to say other than, let's eat and drink."

Instantly, the two women started to serve their meal. The aroma that filled the room when they uncovered the on their plates had Rachel excited to eat. Before they started to dig into their meal, Becky made a toast to their gracious host, and it made Grace blush. They quickly drank their alcohol and started to eat. She hadn't realized how hungry she was until the food on her plate was nearly gone. After months of mostly Ramen noodles, the twins were thankful to have such a well-prepared meal for a change.

Over an hour had passed, and they had all finished their meal. They had toasted several times to almost anything they could think of. Wealth, friendship, happiness, and family. They were all mixed in at one point or another. Though the food was gone, Rachel and the others were all still enjoying the evening. She couldn't remember a recent time that she'd had more fun, and she found herself overjoyed that she hadn't returned to her room.

"So, you guys just travel the country and talk about haunted places?" Zach asked.

"Not always, but sometimes," Becky said. "We just find old properties that have a cool background. Then, we travel to them and film our experience. People love it."

"That's kind of awesome, honestly."

"It totally is. We love being out on the road. I mean, I know it's not for everyone, but I couldn't see us doing anything else. Our followers are really great, too. They've kind of become our family."

"Don't you miss just being in one place?" Grace asked.

"I don't think we really know what that feels like," Rachel said.

"Even when we were kids, we bounced around from home to home. We never really stayed in one place."

The group talked about their travels for a while longer, and then Zach told them some stories about his father. Rachel could tell he had an infatuation with her sister, and Becky didn't push him away, either. The two continued to flirt with one another for most of the night, and she glanced over at Grace to see how she was reacting. Sure enough, the woman definitely looked tense. She didn't want to ruin the evening between the group, so she needed to think fast.

"If you'll give my sister and me a moment, we need to have some time to ourselves. I can't thank you enough for dinner, and it was a pleasure to get time to know the both of you," Rachel said.

"I'm not done spending time with our new friends."

"I know, but we've both had way too much to drink. We have things to do tomorrow."

"We do?" Becky stammered.

Rachel nodded and grabbed her sister by her arm. She smiled at the others, and the twins headed for their rooms. Becky obviously didn't agree with her decision to end the night so early, but it wasn't like her sister had given her a choice. The tension was rising, and the last thing they needed was to start a fight with Grace. She was the only one who had shown even a little kindness to the two of them.

"Why did you do that?" Becky asked.

Rachel sighed. "I know we've had a lot to drink and that you like Zach, but you weren't paying any attention to how Grace felt about it."

"Why should I? The two of them aren't together anymore."

"That's not the point, sis. We need to make friends with these people. We don't need to go around and piss them all off. Besides, whether you can see it or not, there is obviously something still going on between those two. Even if it is one-sided."

They finally made it to Becky's door, and Rachel

opened it and helped her through it. It was easy to see that her sister was still angry with her, but that would wear off with the alcohol by the time she woke up in the morning. Her sister walked through the door and turned around, glaring at her. Without saying a word, Becky slammed the door in her face.

17

Standing at the door that Becky had just slammed in her face, Rachel suddenly realized how drunk she really was. It was the first time since they had started drinking that she was by herself, and the hallway was already spinning. As she glanced down the corridor in the direction of her room, the door seemed to be far away. Putting one foot in front of the other, she started laughing at the ridiculousness of having to teach herself how to walk. Finally, she stumbled into her room and closed the door behind her.

It took several minutes to get her shoes off, but as soon as she did, she toppled onto her bed back first. She was staring at the ceiling, trying to get the world to quit spinning, when she remembered the journal they had found. In the moment they'd had after leaving the library before meeting with Zach and Grace, she had rushed to her room and shoved it under her pillow. Rachel quickly scampered up from her bed and grabbed for it, pulling it out in a single try.

She struggled to open the binder but finally did and celebrated her success. It was at that moment that Rachel knew she'd had more than she should have to drink. Neither of the twins was much in the way of drinkers, but they never turned it down during a social event. There were only a handful of times she had been too drunk to see straight, but that night was slowly reaching the top of that list. Looking down at the journal, the words were all blurry.

Rachel wanted nothing more than to read through the pages and not stop, but it was going to be a difficult task with the effects of the alcohol kicking in full force. Still, she tried to read the same passage she had read earlier in the evening. Making it through the first couple of sentences, she quickly dozed off. Over the next thirty minutes, she woke up half a dozen times before dozing back to sleep. Each time she woke up, she was startled. There was a constant feeling that someone was watching her, but she was too tired to look around the room.

Long before the sun came out, Rachel woke up in a cold sweat. She couldn't remember any kind of dream she was having, but the feeling of waking up to a night terror was real. Quickly opening her eyes and stretching out of bed, she was stunned to find a spirit sitting on the edge of her mattress. The sight alone terrified her. Even as she tried to scream, no sound came out of her mouth. She struggled to get as far away from the entity as she could. Climbing to the top section of her bed and curling her legs under her chin, she studied the ghastly figure at the footboard.

The spirit was a woman with a slight build and translucent. Rachel knew if she reached her hand out, it would have gone right through the woman. The clothes she wore looked to be from the early nineties, and there was a way about her that made her feel like it was safe to talk to her.

"Hello?" Rachel whispered. "Who are you?"

The woman said nothing, but her mouth started to move. For a moment, she wanted to scream again, but the whispering sound coming from the ghost put her at ease. She seemed to be lost, or it was possible she didn't know where she was. Either way, Rachel didn't know what else to do besides getting closer to see if she could understand what the spirit was saying.

"My babies," she whispered. "My little babies need me. Where did my babies go? They need their mother. I'm here for you, my darling angels."

With a start, Rachel bolted straight up in her bed. It took several minutes of looking around the room before she realized it was all just another dream. In her mind, it had all been so real. The emotions of the apparition seemed to seep into her mind. The cold air of the spirit being next to her was almost like she could feel it. Glancing around the room again, she felt a chill run up her arm. She quickly noticed the window was open.

Rachel knew it was closed when she came into the room. She never liked to sleep in a room that had an open window. Her heart started to race at the thought of someone coming into her room through the opening. Slowly, she got up and walked across the room. Glancing out over the property, she reveled in how beautiful it looked, even in the early morning hours. The sun hadn't made it up, and it was still mostly dark aside from the stars and moon lighting up certain areas of the estate.

Suddenly, she saw the woman from her dream walking down the path to the cemetery. Rachel rubbed her eyes to make sure she wasn't just seeing things, but when she opened them again, the lady was still there. Though startled, she was intrigued by what the woman was doing. She didn't waste any time thinking about it and quickly decided to follow her.

Throwing on her shoes and grabbing her phone, she raced toward the bedroom door. She stopped and looked back around the room before going back in and grabbing the journal. A moment later, she had run down the hallway and was flying out the front door. There was no telling what she was getting herself into, but curiosity had gotten the best of her. As quickly as she made it to the backyard, the spirit was gone. Rachel cursed under her breath for going back to grab the journal. If she hadn't wasted that small amount of time hesitating, she wouldn't have lost her.

A moment later, Rachel spotted the figure

moving closer to the cemetery. Adrenaline took over, and she found herself running through the backyard. Making sure she was holding onto the journal tightly, she pulled out her phone and turned on the built-in flashlight. The farther she got from the house, the darker it was.

Just as she reached the beginning of the cemetery, she thought the spirit was gone again. Looking to her left and right, she still couldn't see where it had gone. Rachel was trying to catch her breath when she caught a glimpse of the ghost disappearing behind the crypt. She took her time maneuvering the other headstones scattered everywhere and made her way to the other side herself. She quickly discovered the spirit standing over a grave before it looked back at her and disappeared.

Rachel didn't know what to think. While she had always believed in spirits and ghosts, there wasn't a single time she could remember actually seeing one. Though it was gone for good, she looked around before moving forward. Slowly making her way to the headstone she had last seen the spirit standing over, her heart was racing. When she finally made it to the spot where the ghost had disappeared, she looked down and read her mother's name, along with the normal information written on it.

Shaking her head, Rachel did a double take. The information had to be wrong. According to the dates engraved on the headstone, their mother had been alive for three months after the twins' birth. It didn't make any sense to her. If Amanda had been alive for that long after giving birth, why had they never been placed with her? Even at a young age, the mother would be the first person the hospital would have sent them home with.

She didn't understand what it meant, but she was determined to find out. Quickly pulling out her phone, she opened the camera and snapped a picture of the information. There had to be some kind of explanation for the mistake, and if it wasn't a mistake, then why had they always been told a different story?

Rachel tried to make sense of it all as she made her way back to the house. The ghost had freaked her out, but it hadn't scared her in a way that made her fearful of another visit. Who was the woman, and why had she led her to that grave? Her mind was racing with a million questions, none of which she could answer.

By the time she had made her way out of the small cemetery, she had picked up the pace. The whole thing was starting to freak her out the more she thought about it. She suddenly wanted to know what other lies they had been told. With every noise the wind made, her pace became quicker. Being out on the estate at night and alone scared her. She wanted nothing more than to be back in her bed, but she had questions that needed to be answered.

18

The next morning, Rachel woke up feeling the effects of not getting much sleep the night before. There wasn't a chance to think about what she had seen, though, as Becky was already sitting on the edge of the bed with a smile on her face and two cups of coffee in her hands. She yawned and reached for the cup her sister had extended to her.

"Well, you know how to wake a girl up properly," Rachel said.

"I just wanted to apologize for being such a brat last night. I woke up this morning feeling awful about the way I acted."

"It's okay. I know we all had a little too much to drink. I was only trying to salvage the situation the best way I could."

Becky smiled. "I have to admit, I do remember being a little too wrapped up in Zach to see how

Grace felt. Still, I don't understand why she was acting that way."

"I guess she's not over him as much as he is over her, but I got the vibe that he might still be into her, too. No one gets that jealous over a friend."

"Maybe they still offer each other the benefits of dating without the actual dating."

Rachel laughed. "That could be the case, but I needed to get you out of there before she went off and we had a fight on our hands."

"Thank you for that," Becky said. "How'd you sleep?"

"Not very well. I decided to get up, and I took a walk to the cemetery."

"Why wouldn't you just wait till this morning?"

She wanted to tell her sister about the spirit, but she stopped herself. There was no chance Becky would believe what had happened, so she kept it out of the story as she told her about the rest of her walk to the crypt. She couldn't come up with a good reason to tell her why she went, so she went with the only thing her mind could come up with.

"I just couldn't get to sleep and needed to take a walk to get some fresh air. Besides, when I was walking through the headstones, I found our mom's and took a picture of it. Something isn't right about the timeframe."

Pulling out her phone and opening the image from the night before, Rachel showed her sister the picture of their mother's headstone. There was a moment when neither one of them spoke. They both agreed they needed to do some research on the matter, and they hoped Jessica would come through with the spare key to the crypt.

"Something we can do until Jessica gets the key, or we cut the lock to the crypt, is go to the library."

"I don't remember seeing anything about our family history in the library, but I suppose it wouldn't hurt to look again," Rachel said.

Becky laughed. "I didn't mean the family library. What I meant was that we could drive back to the village and visit the one there. I saw a library and what looked to be a small newspaper business when we were there yesterday. I'm sure with enough digging, we can find something about Mom there."

"I guess if anyone would have information about her, it would be one of them. Though, I think it's kind of weird that neither Mary nor Jessica mentioned Amanda being buried in the cemetery."

"I wouldn't look too much into the whole thing. It could have just slipped their mind, or they really didn't know."

Rachel sighed. "Maybe, but I still wouldn't be surprised if they were hiding something. I don't know that I really trust either one of them, and they definitely don't like each other."

Her sister started to laugh and nodded. It was nice to see that she wasn't the only one who noticed that Mary and Jessica didn't get along. Rachel was excited to get the day started and head back to the local village. While it didn't offer all the benefits of the bigger city, the small newspaper and library could hold the answers to the questions they both had.

Suddenly, there was a knock on the door, and it startled Rachel. She nearly spilled her coffee, but to her surprise, her sister didn't notice. There was a moment that went by when she didn't understand why she was jumpy until the thought of the spirit sitting on her bed jumped back into her mind. Shaking it off, she called out for whoever had knocked to come in. A few seconds later, Grace was standing in the doorway, smiling.

"I figured after last night's events, you'd both be a little hungry. You're welcome to join me for breakfast."

"That sounds great," Becky exclaimed.

She couldn't have agreed with her sister more. Breakfast did sound pretty good, as would anything that would soak up the alcohol from the night before. The twins both jumped up and followed the woman downstairs and into the dining room. As soon as she walked into the room, the energy shifted. She was no longer excited about the idea of breakfast when she noticed Jessica sitting in the parlor.

The one night they had gotten without the woman was great, but now she was right there in front of them. Rachel felt a bit of confusion when Jessica smiled at her and quickly got up to greet them. Nothing the woman did felt fake, but it threw her off a bit after the way she had treated them since their arrival.

"I'm glad to see both of you here together," Jessica

said. "I feel like I should probably apologize for the way I acted yesterday. It was already a bad day, and after hearing Patricia's last will and testament...I don't know. I just miss my friend, and I was just flooded with emotion. I shouldn't have taken it out on you."

Becky smiled. "I understand that. You shouldn't have to deal with us being thrown upon you like this."

"It's what she wanted, but I guess I wasn't as prepared as I thought. I'll do better from now on. Now, how'd the two of you sleep your first night here?"

She still didn't know what to think of the woman, so she kept to herself and smiled politely. Becky, on the other hand, seemed to be bouncing up and down. Her sister was the more cheerful of the two, but mainly because she didn't share the same empath ability that Rachel had. Her emotions were always in turmoil because they would mix with the people around her.

After some light chit-chat, the women shared more coffee. Rachel had to admit the coffee was a blessing, no matter who was serving it. She still had reservations about Jessica and her daughter, but she played nice and put on a good show. While still being cautious with what she said, Rachel was able to make the women feel comfortable without giving off vibes of distrust. It was a curse and a blessing to have that kind of ability, but at that moment, she was thankful for it.

"I know it's all still new for the two of you, but have you thought about your plans yet?" Jessica asked.

"Not really," Rachel said. "We still have time to decide what we want to do."

"Oh, I know, dear. I was just wondering what you are thinking of doing when those six weeks are over."

"We haven't decided fully yet," Becky said. "But I know we both want to keep traveling."

"What about the house?"

"If you guys are on the road traveling, I wouldn't have any problem with staying here and keeping an eye on things," Grace added.

Becky grinned. "I think that would be a great idea. That way, we can always have the house to fall back on."

"We haven't figured everything out. We're going to have to think about it all. I still need to talk to a financial advisor to see what our best course of action is," Rachel said. "It is an idea that we will look into."

Instantly, the room grew quiet. Rachel knew she had struck a nerve, but she wasn't sure who she could trust. Plus, she wasn't sold on the idea of strangers looking after the property while they were away. Becky was trying to ease the tension by being her charming self, but nothing she did seemed to bring the room back to life. Jessica and Grace were lost in their own cups of coffee until Jessica stood up suddenly and looked right at her.

"Would it be all right if you and I had a conversation in private?" Jessica asked.

Rachel felt sick to her stomach and swallowed hard. There was no telling what the woman wanted to say, but she nodded and followed her out of the room.

19

Rachel followed the woman to the front porch. While there was a feeling of tension in the air, she had known from the beginning that they were going to have to have a conversation at some point. When Jessica opened the front door, the sun felt warm on her skin. The warm morning sun and fresh dew on the grass brought with it a refreshing smell she couldn't ignore. Even with her not knowing what was about to be said, she felt at ease.

"I didn't mean to startle you by thrusting that on you, but I just think it's past time for us to have a talk about things," Jessica said.

"I couldn't agree more. I feel like there has been some confusion about what part we play here at the estate."

"Not on my end, though I apologize for making you feel like there has been. I know the property and everything on it is yours and your sister's, but you have to understand how rough it has been since Patricia passed. She was a good friend, and she meant a lot to me."

Rachel sighed. "I get that, but nothing has to change for you. Other than the fact that she's gone, we're not here to make drastic changes. This is all new to us, too. We know nothing about our family history."

"Well, I hope you can find the answers you're looking for."

"Me too. You can start by telling me exactly how Patricia died."

Jessica paused and then sighed. "You know, she never wanted to grow old and frail. As I said before, Patricia was a strong woman, and for her, the idea of growing old meant she would have to admit that she was getting weaker. It wasn't something she could live with."

"What are you saying?"

"I'm saying that no matter how strong the woman was when it came to her mind slipping, she couldn't handle it. Eventually, she just gave up, and that was when Patricia took her own life."

She was stunned by the statement. Instantly, Rachel felt horrible for bringing it up. If she had known Patricia had committed suicide, she never would have asked about it. Still, it was shocking to hear that the powerful woman everyone around knew had been reduced to taking her own life in the end. She knew everyone had their limit, but that was never something she would do to herself.

Rachel looked around the property, trying to find the words to apologize. It was obvious by her reaction that Jessica had really cared for the woman and that the two must have been close. For Patricia to have brought the woman into her house to care for her in her final days, there had to have been some kind of good relationship between the two.

"I didn't mean to bring it up like that, but I didn't know."

Jessica shrugged. "It's not your fault, but now you do."

"What was it that you wanted to talk about?" Rachel asked.

"Honestly, I just wanted to say that I know I'm not welcome here anymore. So, I'll be staying at the bed and breakfast in town."

"That's not true. You're more than welcome to stay here for as long as you'd like. My sister and I aren't coming here to kick anyone out."

"Maybe, but I feel like I have overstayed my welcome. If there is anything you need from me, you know where I'll be."

"It is your choice on what you decide to do, but you should know you are welcome here."

"That's okay. It's hard enough to be in the same house that Patricia was in for so long. I only ask that you let Grace stay. The only thing I care about in the world is my daughter. I promise it will only be long enough for me to find a suitable place for the two of us to move," Jessica pleaded.

"Well, that's not going to be a problem at all. If you change your mind, you're welcome to come back and stay at the estate," Rachel said. "Your daughter can stay for as long as she wants to or until you find a place."

Jessica nodded and turned her head to look out over the property. The beautiful morning was just getting started, but Rachel felt like it was some kind of ending for the woman. It was touching to hear Jessica talk about her daughter. She never knew how much they really cared for each other as mother and daughter, but she had never experienced that bond. Still, even after all the things the woman had done in the past day, she felt bad that Jessica was going to be leaving them.

"I appreciate you letting Grace stay. I'm going to go upstairs and pack a few things, and then I'll be out of your hair."

"I know I can't talk you out of it, but I want you to know we have no problem with you being here. We're all just getting to know each other, and we still have so many questions."

"I know, but I think it's for the best."

Rachel tried a few more times to talk Jessica out of leaving. No matter what had transpired between the two, there was no reason she had to leave. She was right when she said that they were just getting to know each other. As with any relationship, there were bound to be disagreements and arguments.

Still, no matter how hard she tried to talk Jessica into staying at the house, the woman was adamant about leaving.

The house was suddenly starting to feel darker than it had before, and she felt like she had done something wrong just by being there. Though the property was more beautiful than ever, the sun wasn't shining on her heart. Jessica smiled at her and headed back into the house to pack. There was no getting through to the woman that there weren't any hard feelings, and Rachel walked into the house and back to the parlor.

It was a happy sight she walked into when she saw her sister and Grace joking around and laughing. Rachel wished she could join in the fun, but she suddenly found herself not in the mood for their company. Not wanting to interrupt, she decided to go back to her room. While she was glad the two were hitting it off so well, she still couldn't get over the conversation she'd had with Jessica.

There had been a sadness in the woman's voice, and Rachel felt like it was her fault she was leaving. Still, she did everything she could to make her stay. It was Jessica's decision to make, and it was obvious she had made it. She took her time climbing the stairs before making the turn down the hallway toward her room. Suddenly, her gut started to twist, and she knew something wasn't right.

Hearing a noise she couldn't quite make out, Rachel stopped in the hallway and strained to hear. A whispering voice was coming from down the hall.

The whispering and cursing continued for several moments, and she became worried that something was wrong with Jessica.

Without giving it a second thought, she rushed down the hall to check on the woman. Even if Jessica was leaving, it didn't mean that Rachel didn't care what happened to her. The older woman had poured her heart out to her, and she wanted to make sure nothing was wrong.

The sounds weren't coming from Jessica's room, though, and she was stunned when she turned in the direction of the library and found the door cracked open. Maybe it wasn't the person she thought it was, after all. Trying to be as quiet as possible, Rachel made her way to the door and peered through the opening. Immediately, she could see Jessica moving things around like she was looking for something in particular. The soft cursing continued.

As soon as she saw the woman reaching for the book that would open the door to the hidden office, Rachel made her move and knocked on the door. She could see she had startled Jessica when she walked through the door and smiled. Without saying a word, Jessica quickly adjusted herself and brushed past Rachel and back into the hallway, leaving her to wonder what she could have been looking for. Before completely disappearing into her room, she turned back to her.

"I was just trying to find a book for my afternoon reading," Jessica offered.

Rachel didn't say anything, and she watched as

the woman returned to her room and closed the door. It was a good explanation for being in the library, but the fact that she had been reaching for the hidden switch to the office meant there was no way Jessica had been telling the truth.

20

Rachel was sitting in her room when Jessica was getting ready to leave the house. Though she had started to believe their relationship had made a jump in the right direction, the feeling was quickly dashed when she had caught her snooping around the library moments later. Grace and Becky had both come to her room to ask her if she was going to come to see Jessica off, but she didn't want to.

A short time after that, both the girls came back to her room to ask if Rachel wanted to go with them to the village to shop. Becky was shocked when she simply shrugged and said she was going to stay back and do some editing for the blog.

"Are you sure you don't want to go?" Becky asked.

"I'm sure, sis. You guys go and have a good time. I've got some photos that need to be edited for the website, and I really would like to just hang out by myself for a little while."

"That can wait until later. We're going to have a lot to put on the blog within the next few days anyway. You should go with us. I think it would be good if we all spent some time together."

Rachel smiled. "We'll have plenty of time to hang out over the next few weeks. You go, and if you see something you think I'd enjoy, bring it back with you."

Her sister laughed. "Fine, but I think you're going to be missing out."

She shrugged and watched the two girls trot out of her room. It was easy to see that Grace and Becky were getting along. As nice as it sounded to go on a shopping trip with the both of them, she had her mind on something else entirely. She wasn't about to do any editing on photos for the blog. Instead, she wanted to snoop around in Patricia's office a little more and read the woman's journal.

As soon as she heard the girls pulling out of the driveway, she made her way downstairs and got herself another cup of coffee. She made a mental note to find out what brand the coffee was since it was the best coffee she'd ever tasted. Which wasn't saying much since she was used to filtered coffee on the road in an old RV. After pouring her cup, she rushed upstairs to the library and pulled the lever. The door to the hidden office opened, and Rachel went inside.

The room was still filled with dust, but it smelled

better than it had the day before. Taking a seat at the desk, she immediately started to rummage through the drawers. In the first one, she found a few old photos. They were random, but it was still nice to look through the pictures of her grandmother. One of the pictures had Patricia with both Mary and Jessica. It was strange to see the three women together looking as happy as they did, but the image had been taken years earlier.

There was no way of knowing what had transpired between the group that had caused a rift between Mary and Jessica. Still, the one picture she was hoping to find wasn't there. Rachel still had no idea who the ghost had been, but she had thought it could be their mother, Amanda. She was hoping to find one of her, but out of all the images she looked through, there were none. In several of the pictures she had looked at, there was a man she had never seen. Quickly, she wondered who he was to her grandmother.

After not finding what she was hoping to find in the pictures, Rachel sat back in the chair and pulled open Patricia's journal. It still amazed her to see how beautiful her grandmother's handwriting was. Flipping through the pages, she started to read several of the entries.

There are those who speak of the beauties of childbirth and the months that the infant is carried within you. For me, though, it would seem the ability to glow with the rays of joy is lost. Each time I try to stand or walk the gardens, I'm almost instantly doubled over in pain or vomiting in the most disturbing fashion. It will be worth it in the end when I'm holding our precious baby. My dear husband and I have tried for so long.

The joy I saw in my lover's eyes was unlike any I'd known before. He doesn't know about the hardships I've endured during the pregnancy. There is no reason for him to know about my suffering; it would only bring him sorrow, and that's the last thing I want. It's only a few more weeks. Then we'll have our precious baby, and the world will once again be in perfect balance.

The entry ended. Rachel's eyes moved down to the bottom of the page. When she flipped to the next one, nearly two months had passed for Patricia.

Looking back, it's hard to see the joy in my words. While my beautiful girl has joined the world, it's bittersweet. My beloved Frederick was taken from us in the most terrible way. He was walking with our sweet child in the stroller before him when suddenly, his heart gave out. While the doctors assured me it was a heart attack, I'm certain his heart failed from growing with love for our daughter. Had it not been for my dear friends Mary and Jessica, I don't know how I would have survived these past four weeks.

Rachel frowned, rereading the passage again. It didn't make any sense. Jessica had told her that she'd only known Patricia for a few years, yet the proof was right there in her grandmother's writings and photographs. Something wasn't adding up. Before she could dive back into the journal, a knock on the front door echoed through the halls.

Not wanting anyone else to know about the

office, she grabbed the journal and headed out the door, forgetting her cup of coffee in the process. Rachel rushed to the front door, expecting to find Mary being the one knocking. She was the only other person they had met since arriving and the only one who could be trying to gain access to the house. When Rachel swung open the door, she was shocked to see her on-again, off-again boyfriend, Josh Allen, standing in front of her.

"What are you doing here?" Rachel asked, still reeling.

"You know I still follow your blog, even if we aren't together. I was watching it last night and saw that you and Becky were here at the estate."

"That still doesn't quite answer the question, Josh. What are you doing here?"

Josh sighed. "Well, I saw the two of you were here, and I know the area and house well. I figured I would check in on you and see how things were coming along. I was worried about you."

"You were worried about me, but you couldn't just pick up the phone and call to see if I was all right?"

"It's not the same thing to check on someone over the phone. Besides, I wanted to see you."

Rachel wasn't sure how to feel about him being there, but she invited him, nonetheless. No matter the reason for his arrival at the estate, it would be nice to have another person she knew to share her experience with. Though the two of them were not currently together, they had always remained close in the way friends usually do. They walked through the house, stopping to grab a few beers to take with them before settling on the chairs on the back porch.

The conversation started with her explaining the way the RV had caught on fire and how they had ended up at a local motel for the night. He smiled and nodded through everything she told him about James showing up and telling them about the inheritance. Rachel was feeling good about having Josh there to talk to. The man had always been a great listener.

She was enjoying the idea of having someone there to talk to. He continued to listen to every word she said as she told him about the women they had met at the estate and how things were going overall. Rachel blushed when his hand reached out and took hers. The moment his hand touched hers, she could feel the sparks ignite inside of her. Her heart was racing, and the chemistry between the pair was easy to see.

It didn't matter how much time they ever spent apart. Deep down in her heart, she knew he was the one. Rachel quickly forgot everything going on in an instant. She melted at his touch. Josh, for all his faults, would always be her soulmate. As they settled on the parlor sofa, Rachel wondered what to make of his sudden appearance.

21

Rachel found herself wanting to tell Josh about everything. The man meant more to her than she could have ever imagined, and the idea of finally having someone besides her sister to talk to about everything made her feel giddy. The pair were sipping on their second beer each, and she slowly began relaxing enough to open up to him.

"You know, I've been learning so much about Patricia through this journal I found."

Josh smiled. "That's amazing. All this time, you didn't know about your family, only to find out that your grandmother had all of this and left it for you."

"It's not all it's cracked up to be. It's been quite the trip, that's true, but the woman here are all at each other's throats in one way or another. Something happened between Mary and Jessica, but I have no idea what," Rachel said.

"I take it the two don't get along very well."

"Not at all. Then, for some unknown reason,

Jessica went and left the estate. I tried to talk her into staying, but she wasn't having any of it."

"Well, I'm sure she feels like she's being kicked out of the house that she's been living in for several years now."

Rachel scoffed. "Maybe, but I told her she was welcome to stay for as long as she wanted. Still, nothing made her want to stay. It's all just kind of weird. Plus, Jessica lied about how long she had known Patricia. The three of them have been friends for a long time, so I don't understand why she wouldn't be honest about it."

"I'm sure there's something we can do to figure out what happened and even why she didn't tell the truth. I'll help you figure it out as best as I can, but I think we should start with the newspaper. Maybe there was some incident that took place that caused the turn."

Rachel laughed. "Honestly, I had the same idea myself."

"Hell, it's a beautiful day out, and we're enjoying our time together. I think we can manage to get to the newspaper and check it out now if you'd like."

For a moment, Rachel didn't know what to say. She was blown away by how he had been so receptive to everything she said. Now, with the level of excitement he was expressing to help her, she was nearly overjoyed. While Becky was willing to let her go through and figure out the mystery in everything, she still enjoyed living her life more. With the possibility of sharing the findings with her new partner, she smiled at the man standing in front of her.

"That's a great idea," Rachel said. "Give me a few minutes, and I'll be ready to go."

He smiled. "Sounds good to me." He smiled.

After grabbing her phone, she sent her sister a quick message. She didn't want Becky to be caught off guard if they ran into her in the village. Even as excited as she had been to learn about her grandmother, it didn't compare to how she felt about Josh being there. It came as quite a surprise when he appeared at her door, but she had come around quickly and was now happy he was there. Not only had the man been a staple in her life off and on, but the two were also great friends.

She smiled as she grabbed her purse and followed Josh from the house. Though the two had shared a couple of drinks, it had been over the course of a few hours, and they were both sober enough to drive. They quickly opted to take his truck. Being the gentleman Josh was, he even opened the door for her as she got into the passenger's seat. She blushed as he closed the door and rushed to the driver's side.

The couple pulled out of the driveway and headed into town. Rachel was instantly happy she had chosen to ride as the passenger again. She couldn't get over how beautiful the area was, and it gave her time to think about everything she had discovered so far.

"One of the things I learned since being here is that my mother passed away three months after we were born," Rachel said. "I went up to the family cemetery, and that was when I found Amanda's headstone. I even took a picture of it for reference."

"That doesn't make any sense. I thought she died giving birth."

"It's something else I wanted to look into at the newspaper. Not only would I like to see what else has happened at the estate, but the big mystery for me now is also figuring out why the date on the grave doesn't match what we were told."

"I understand that. It's a mystery I would like to figure out as well. I'm sure we'll learn something while we're there. They should have all the clippings from the area going back many years."

"That's what I'm hoping."

Josh smiled. "Well, if not, you know you and your sister have a ton of followers. I bet they'd be willing to look into things, too."

"I'd rather not tell anyone about it just yet."

He nodded, and moments later, they were pulling into the village. She was thankful Josh understood how she felt. It wasn't every day a person met someone they had such a connection with. A rush of adrenaline rushed through her when they parked the truck near the newspaper. Something told her they were about to find out everything she wanted to know.

They quickly got out and walked up to the door. Josh rushed to get in front of her to hold the door open, but when he pulled on it, it was locked. Rachel suddenly felt a twinge of disappointment until she looked up in the window and spotted a handwritten sign. Reading over it, she was happy to see that the employees were just out for lunch, meaning they'd be back soon.

"I mean, that sounds like a good idea to me," Josh said. "I could go for some food myself."

Rachel smiled. "I don't see why not. After all, they're probably going to be out for a little while longer, depending on when they left. What sounds good to you?"

"I don't know, but I'm sure we can find something around here."

They both quickly turned around and started walking down the street. Rachel hadn't been to the village enough times to really know what was available, but just the fact that she was there with Josh made everything worth it. Though she was more than anxious to find out all she could about her past, she was enjoying herself as they walked. Suddenly, she spotted Grace and Becky coming toward them.

In a flash, Becky looked up and saw the two walking down the street. Rushing up to both of them, she wrapped her arms around Josh. As many times as Rachel and Josh had been together, he and her sister had built a sibling-like relationship. Even when the two would separate for long periods of time, Becky and Josh still were as close as ever. She smiled as they separated, and Rachel quickly noticed the curiosity in Grace's eyes.

"Grace, this is Josh. We've been dating off and on

over the last several years, and he's come to see how we were doing."

"It's so good to meet you, Josh." Grace grinned.

"Nice to meet you, as well."

Without reason, Rachel caught herself getting jealous of the woman. It was easy to see she was quite smitten with the man standing before them, and even if she didn't want to admit it, she didn't like it one bit.

"Are the two of you hungry?" Becky asked.

"We were actually just getting ready to go to lunch," Josh replied.

"You should totally join us."

Rachel smiled, knowing there wasn't a way to decline the invitation. She would have rather spent her time alone with Josh, but it was likely they'd just end up having lunch at the same place as the other girls. A moment later, the four of them were walking down the street in the direction of a small café. Suddenly, Josh reached down and took Rachel's hand, startling her.

The moment she felt his hand touch hers, Rachel relaxed. As she looked up into his handsome green eyes, she felt assured that Josh only had eyes for her. After all, he had come to see her and no one else. The loving warmth with which he stared at her made her heart melt, and everything else faded away. She quickly glanced ahead when she felt someone looking at them. She gloated slightly when she saw Grace's curious eyes fall upon them. Instantly, the woman's cheeks flushed red.

22

While everyone seemed to be enjoying the meal itself, lunch was intense. The conversation was filled with nothing more than small talk, and Rachel knew part of it was because of her own jealousy. Even though she felt like Josh was committing himself to her when he took her hand, Grace still made things difficult. Her constant flirting was getting on her nerves, but she knew Josh was only trying to be polite with his responses.

"So, Grace, tell me about yourself," Josh said.

She smiled. "Well, there's not much to tell, honestly. I mean, I've lived around here my whole life and have been staying at the estate for the last few years."

"That sounds nice. What about you, Becky? How have things been while traveling?"

"I'm sure Rachel has updated you on all of that, but I have to admit that I've been having a blast updating our followers and interacting with them.

We have the best people you could ask for following our page."

"That's great. I always knew the two of you would take that whole thing someplace special. I'm glad to hear it's working out for you."

Becky laughed. "It's only been about six weeks, Josh Not a whole lot has changed."

"Maybe not, but I've been watching the website. You've added a ton of followers lately."

"That part's true."

They chuckled amongst themselves for a moment longer before the conversation died down again. Rachel was happy to see things hadn't changed between the two, but she was trying to gain enough courage to ask the questions she wanted to know about Grace. As much as she wanted to trust the woman, there was still something that wasn't sitting right with her. Seeing her opening, she took it.

'Grace, I've been wondering how it was for you growing up," Rachel said.

"It's not the greatest story, honestly. My parents split up when I was young. I guess they just couldn't make things work out between them. Still, it was rough for a while, and I lived with my dad until I was about thirteen."

'What happened to make you move back with your mom?"

"My dad passed away, and I really had no other choice at the time," Grace replied.

She instantly felt bad for bringing it up. Though she often let her curiosity get the best of her, there was no way she could have known the woman's father had passed away. Still, Rachel tried to back down and change the direction of the conversation.

"I'm sorry, Grace. I had no idea your life was like that."

Grace sighed. "It is what it is. I really don't feel bad about the way I've lived. I mean, I wish my father was still around, but there's nothing I can do to change that. After he passed away, I moved back to Vermont to stay at the family estate."

"After Vermont, is that when you both moved to Alabama?" Rachel asked.

"Yeah. We sold the estate and decided to move around this area. Not long after that, my mother met Patricia, and then her health started to decline. We moved in with her a short time later and have been staying at the estate since. I only helped with the things that I could help with, but Patricia was such a nice woman that she let us both live there with her."

"Did Jessica ever mention knowing Patricia before that?"

"No, because she never knew her before that. I think you might have her confused with Mary."

Rachel was shocked, but she didn't want to push the woman any further. She quickly dropped the subject, and besides the occasional joke or comment, the rest of the meal went on in silence. She found herself trying to finish eating as quickly as possible so she and Josh could head back to the newspaper office. The awkward conversation was still fresh in her mind, and Rachel couldn't understand the picture she had found on her grandmother's desk that had all three women standing together.

Finally, the four finished eating and left the café. Rachel was looking forward to seeing what they could find in the newspaper, and she was ready to split from her sister and Grace. It wasn't that she didn't enjoy the women's company, but she felt as though she had already pushed the questions far enough.

"You know, Josh, I'd love to show you around time if you're up for it. It's not a very big town, but it has a lot to offer," Grace said.

"I'm anxious to see the village, but I've already made plans with Rachel."

"Yeah, we're going over to the newspaper to do a little research," Rachel said.

"Oh, well, maybe we can all go over there. I wouldn't mind looking up some stuff myself, and if you need any help, I can do that."

Becky scoffed. "That would be a horrible idea."

"What do you mean?"

"We have all that paint and stuff in the car. We've already spent too much time at lunch and might have ruined some of the supplies as it is."

Grace chuckled. "Good call. I nearly forgot about all of it. Maybe next time, Rachel."

Rachel smiled. "That works for us."

Even though Grace spoke as though everything was just fine, Rachel couldn't help but see the way she looked when she realized they couldn't stay. Something still seemed off about the woman, but she didn't know what. Regardless, she played nice with Grace as they all said goodbye. Rachel watched the two leave and start walking to their car. Though she had dodged a bullet that time, she knew it wouldn't be the end of it. As long as Josh was going to be around, she knew she'd have to keep her eyes on Grace. The woman had eyes for him, and she knew it was going to be a problem.

Again, the two made their way back to the newspaper office. Rachel knew they had given the staff more than enough time to finish their lunch and get back to work. Josh took her hand again, and she smiled up at him when he did. She surprised herself by how much she had missed him. They hadn't been apart for very long, but when they had ended the relationship the last time, it hadn't been on bad terms. He had wanted more from their relationship than she was ready to give.

As they arrived at the front door, Josh immediately leaned in front of her and held the door open for her. She couldn't help but admit that she had missed that about him. The two laughed when they walked through the door until she looked up and was stunned to see a familiar face. Standing behind the counter was none other than Mary.

"It's so good to see you again, Rachel," Mary said when she spotted her. "And who, might I ask, is this handsome man you've brought with you?"

Rachel grinned. "This is Josh, and Josh, this here is Mary. She was one of Patricia's oldest friends."

"Oh, it melts my heart to hear that you remembered that. We went way back, that's for sure. What brings you to the newspaper?"

"Well, I was hoping to look at some old articles, but since you're here, maybe you have some time to talk."

Mary looked around the office and made a scene while seeing if there was anyone in the building. After another moment, the woman laughed and shrugged.

"I suppose I could spare a few minutes. Looks like I really have all the time in the world. Why don't the two of you come back to the office and have a seat?"

The pair followed the woman to the office and took a seat on the chairs provided. Rachel was glad to see Mary's more carefree side after witnessing the tense interactions she had with Jessica. After guiding the two of them to the office, Mary disappeared back out the door, leaving them alone in the room.

As with any new place she had ever been, Rachel started looking around the room and all the different pictures on the wall. History was something she had always enjoyed, and the old articles hanging on the wall brought a smile to her face. Whether it was new businesses opening or a fire that had been extinguished forty years ago, she enjoyed reading each one.

"Isn't this amazing?" Rachel asked.

Josh smiled. "It is. I can't believe a small town like this has had so many newsworthy articles. What about that one?"

Rachel's eyes followed his pointing finger to

where another old newspaper clipping was framed on the wall and gasped. It was a picture of the manor in black and white. All the estate's staff were lined up on either side of the porch. Standing there in a maid's uniform was an incredibly young Jessica Frank.

23

There were still a few minutes between when Rachel saw the image and when Mary came walking back in. Rachel was still confused by the clipping, as she had already seen the picture that had all three women on her grandmother's desk. While she had thought the three of them had been friends, it was looking more like Jessica had been an employee at the estate.

"That newspaper picture up on the wall there, that's the estate, right?"

"This?" Mary asked. "It is. Why do you ask?"

"I was looking at it, and I thought the woman right here was Jessica, but that can't be right."

"Oh, it's right. That's definitely her, all right."

Rachel sighed. "Jessica lied to me, then. She said she didn't know you and Patricia for more than the last three years. Why would she feel like she had to lie about something like that?"

"Well, I'm not all that surprised that she would

try to tell you otherwise. Jessica went above and beyond to change everything about who she was."

"Why would she want to do something like that?"

"She worked for the estate all those years ago, but shortly after she left, she married into money. Jessica is a prideful woman, and after making changes to herself, she snagged herself a husband who had family money."

"So, she just didn't want anyone to know what she had done when she was younger?"

"In a way, I guess you could say that. She didn't want people to think less of her. And when she had the money to do whatever she wanted, she made sure everyone forgot about the roots she was really born into."

She sat back in her chair and tried to let everything she'd just discovered settle in. Mary quietly sat next to her and gave Rachel the time she needed to process everything. There were still things that weren't connecting in her mind. While it was normal for people to want to change things about themselves, it almost seemed like Jessica had gone out of her way to change her entire life story.

On the outside, Jessica had tried to make it look like she and Patricia had been friends for only a short time. She had more or less implied that they had met after Jessica had moved to the area and after Patricia had become ill. Jessica had insinuated that was when she moved in to help care for the woman. In reality, it looked as though she had worked at the estate many years before that. Rachel didn't know what to think, but she still had questions. Pulling herself from her thoughts, she glanced back up at Mary.

Mary smiled. "Is there anything else I can try to answer for you? I might not have the answers to everything, but I am a wealth of knowledge. Especially when it comes to your grandmother."

"There is something else, as a matter of fact."

"Well, ask me anything you want. If I know the answer, I'll give it to you," Mary said.

"When Becky and I were born in the hospital, and as we grew older, we were told that our mother died giving birth to us. The thing is, when I went to the cemetery, I found Amanda's headstone. According to the dates at the grave, she actually died three months later."

"I wouldn't know anything about that."

"Why is that?"

Mary sighed. "Unfortunately, a few days before Amanda showed up, your grandmother and I had a falling out. We went a short time without talking to each other. It wasn't until Amanda's funeral that we finally started speaking again."

Rachel was shaken, but she was still determined to get answers. She wasn't sure what to think about all of it. At first, when she first saw the dates on the headstone, she simply thought there had been a mistake. Why else would they have been lied to for their entire life? Still, she pushed her doubts to the side. There was too much to discuss, and the one question she wanted to be answered was on the tip of her tongue.

"I don't know if you'll be able to tell me this, but how did my mother die?"

"It was a tragic accident that took us all by surprise. It was right after winter, and the river was high due to the melting of all the snow. Amanda got too close to the edge and fell in. She was quickly swept under and dragged down the river. Your mother drowned in a matter of minutes, from what the coroner said."

"I...that's an awful way to go," Josh said. "I'm sorry you had to learn it this way."

"It's not like I didn't know she was gone, but I was always told she died at the hospital when we were born."

Josh took her hand and squeezed it. She was glad he had been there when Mary had told her how her mother had really passed away, but the news was still devastating. Her mother's drowning in the river wasn't what she had expected to hear, and she took a deep breath before releasing it slowly. Learning Amanda's fate was one thing, but it brought another question to mind.

"Why didn't Patricia ever come looking for us? I mean, she knew we were out there, but it wasn't until she died that we learned about her."

"I wish I could answer that for you," Mary said. "She never talked about it."

"You mentioned that before my mother came

back, you and Patricia had a falling out," Rachel said. "What was it about?"

Mary shook her head. "It all seems really silly now. Looking back at everything we went through, it almost doesn't seem real. Patricia had accused me of stealing some stupid key. I can deal with being called a lot of things, but being called a thief is not one of them. I would never steal from anyone."

"What happened with the two of you after that?" Rachel asked. "I assume the two of you worked things out."

"Well, it was months later, and I guess Patricia found it. I was at home when she stopped by, begging me to forgive her. She apologized, and I couldn't go without doing so. After all, she was my best friend, and we all make mistakes. After that, we promised each other never to fight over something so trivial again. We never did. Even if we had different opinions on something, we didn't fight. It made our relationship stronger."

Rachel was quickly blown away. Something so simple had caused such a great rift in their friendship. She had come to get answers, and she was getting them, but at a great cost. It didn't seem real that they had been lied to about their mother, but part of her was glad she knew the truth now. Still, the reason their grandmother never came for them was a mystery on its own. The room fell silent as they could all tell she was deep in her own thoughts. Rachel nearly didn't notice anyone was still in the room until Josh squeezed her hand again, pulling her back to the present.

"I'm glad you told me about my mother. I don't know if I would have been able to find out on my own," Rachel said.

"Any time, sweetheart. Your grandmother was an amazing woman, and I wish you would have gotten the chance to know her before she passed."

"I do wonder, however, if that key that Patricia lost is the same key that opens the crypt. Makes me wonder what is inside again."

Mary smiled. "The family archives should be in there if I remember correctly, but I'm sure you knew that. You'll probably find a lot more answers if you go into the crypt and take a look."

Rachel sighed. "I'm sure it will answer several questions, but I still have to get the key from Jessica."

She watched as the woman's smile faded and was replaced by a confused looked. Rachel wondered what was on Mary's mind and what she could have said that had brought it up. For a moment, she didn't know what to say. The two women looked at each other in confusion for several seconds before she decided to speak first.

"Is everything all right?"

"Why would Jessica have the key?" Mary asked.

"I don't know, but when I asked about it, she said she would have to find the spare, since the original had been lost a long time ago. Now, I'm just waiting for her to give me the spare."

Mary scoffed. "I think she's lying to you about that as well. See, Patricia hid that key a long time ago to keep people from getting ahold of it. As far as I know, she never told a soul where it was. Jessica should never have had the key, and there certainly was never a spare."

24

A strange sensation came over her as she thought about all the things the woman was telling her. She sat for a minute, trying to understand what would make Jessica think she had to lie about everything, but she knew there wasn't anything more that Mary could tell her. As she started to think about getting into the crypt, Rachel couldn't help but wonder if her grandmother had hidden the key in the same office where she had found the journal.

Her thoughts began to drift to when she had walked in on Jessica trying to get into the same office and quickly took off when Rachel had announced herself. What was the woman really trying to do? She didn't want to say anything else to the woman, and she was grateful to get all the answers Mary had given her.

After thanking Mary repeatedly, she and Josh left

the office and headed for his truck. Rachel was still confused about several things, and in many ways, she left with more questions. A few minutes later, the two of them were driving back to the estate. She was in a haze while trying to figure out what everything meant, and it wasn't until she heard Josh's voice that she was able to pull herself back to the ride.

'You look like you're lost in thought, though I fully understand it after learning about how your mom really passed. Is there anything I can do to help? Do you want to talk about something?"

'I don't know. It was a lot to take in, but I just don't understand why Jessica would lie about so many things. It's not making any sense."

"Maybe she just thought it would be easier for you to believe that the key was lost rather than tell you your grandmother had hidden it."

Rachel sighed. "You're an optimist, but I don't think she would even know about it being hidden somewhere if my grandmother was trying to keep it from everyone."

"What are you going to do?" Josh asked.

"Well, I'm certainly going to look for the answers. I found the journal in a secret office behind a wall in the library. I was thinking the key to the crypt might be hiding in there."

"Hell, let's go back to the house and check it out. I bet that's right where it is, and we'll find those answers for you."

She smiled at his enthusiasm. Even though he had

surprised her by showing up, she couldn't have been happier about him coming. Things were going so well that she thought about telling Josh about the ghost. No one else would believe her, but he might. Quickly thinking about what everyone else's reaction would have been, Rachel changed her mind and kept quiet. Maybe, after they had spent a little more time together, she'd explain what she had seen.

A few minutes later, they were pulling into the estate. While the day hadn't gone exactly as she had hoped, she was happy to have gotten a few answers from Mary. The woman was full of knowledge and seemed willing to answer all her questions. Rachel was glad they had gone to the newspaper while she had been there. It was a blessing to have caught her during the time they decided to go.

Just as Josh brought the truck to a stop, Rachel saw Becky sitting on the porch. Next to her was Grace, but after the rest of the day slowly passed, she felt better about the woman than she had earlier. The pair quickly joined the two women on the porch. Everyone seemed happy to see one another, but Josh didn't hesitate to excuse himself, claiming he needed to get settled in.

She knew he was trying to keep his distance from Grace, but that almost made her more comfortable with the two being around each other. Before she and Josh could make their way into the house, Grace stopped them. Taking a deep breath, Rachel turned around.

"You guys should join us for dinner. It's going to be a little later, but it would be nice for all of us to hang out again."

Rachel nodded, but she knew Grace was staring at Josh. There was a comfort between them that she didn't like, even though she was starting to get used to it from Grace. She was staring at him with a big smile, like Rachel wasn't even there. Rachel had to step between them before agreeing to dinner. They quickly made their way into the house, up the stairs, and into her bedroom. A moment later, they slipped down the hall and into the library, closing the door so no one could see.

When she reached up and pulled the lever behind the fake book on the shelf, the gears clicked into action, and the false shelves slowly clicked open. Josh stood in place for several moments, stunned by what he had just seen.

"You know, if we weren't in a hurry, I'd love to figure out how that thing works," Josh said.

"Yeah? Why's that?"

He smiled. "I've always been a sucker for antiques and things like that. Plus, the creepy nature of the place brings a whole new level to everything I just love."

"That makes two of us then, but I'd rather not let Grace know about this little secret, so we need to get moving."

"I understand wanting to keep it all a secret, but why would you keep it from Grace? You haven't mentioned the same kind of problems with her as you have with her mother."

"I really don't know how close she is to Jessica, and I really don't want that woman to know we've been in here."

Rachel rushed into the office and started rummaging through everything. Quickly rifling through the desk drawers, she found an envelope with pictures and two more journals, but there wasn't a key to be seen. While she knew her grandmother would have picked a better hiding place, she was hoping to find it quickly.

"Dammit," Rachel said.

"No luck, I'm guessing," he replied.

"It's not here, but—"

Before she could finish her sentence, Rachel heard someone coming up the stairs. Still not wanting to get caught in the office or even let anyone know it was there, she quickly slipped out of the room and closed the hidden door. She had the envelope and both journals under her arm as she and Josh took a seat at the table in the center of the library. There was no telling what she would find when she opened them, but curiosity was getting the best of her when she decided to pull the photos from the envelope and go through them.

As the two were looking at each picture, Rachel couldn't help but almost be brought to tears when she found one of Patricia and a young woman. She quickly closed her eyes and tried not to cry when she realized the woman would have been about the twins' age. Immediately, there was a recognition that the woman was her mother, Amanda. Though she couldn't be sure until she turned the photo around and read the back. Sure enough, the photo was of their mother and grandmother, dated roughly two months after their birth.

Rachel couldn't believe it as she brushed a wayward tear from her cheek. For the first time, she was looking at a memory between Patricia and her mother. It was a tender moment. Josh reached over and put his arm around her, knowing how important it was. Suddenly, there was a knock on the door, which startled her. In a panic, she tucked the pictures back into the envelope and tried to tuck the envelope under the journals.

In her rush, she mistakenly tipped the envelope upside down, and all the images poured out on the table, but something else dropped into her hand. Looking down, Rachel couldn't believe what she was holding. It was the key they had been looking for. She quickly looked back at Josh in a panic, and he touched his chest.

Instantly, she knew what he was telling her to do. Just as the door started to creak open, Rachel shoved her hand into her shirt and tucked the key into her bra. Pulling her hand back out just in time, it seemed, as the door fully opened, and Jessica was standing in front of them. The woman was smiling at first, but as she looked around, it quickly faded.

It didn't take Rachel long to figure out why the woman suddenly seemed so upset. Lying on the table in front of them were two journals and a bunch of old pictures. Slowly, Jessica's gaze traveled from the table back to Rachel, with her eyes narrowing when their eyes met. She couldn't tell if the look she was getting was one of anger or resentment.

25

"I thought you were going to be staying in town," Rachel said. "I wasn't expecting you to be here?"

"I forgot a few things and wanted to grab them while I had the chance. I didn't mean to barge in like that, but I did knock first."

She didn't believe the woman for a moment, but she knew until she could figure out what Jessica's real intentions were that she was going to have to play nice. It was easy to see the woman was more worried about the items sitting in front of them than she was about the couple actually sitting there. Rachel couldn't be sure, but there was something off about the way she was being so nice.

"Oh, it's not a problem. I already told you that you're welcome to stay here if you want."

Jessica smiled. "That's nice of you, but I still think that my staying in town is for the best. Maybe if I felt a little better about everything, it would be different."

"Well, if you change your mind, just let me know. Is there something I can help you with?"

"No, I just thought I'd try to find a book while I was here. I didn't expect to find you in the library."

Rachel chuckled. "We're just passing the time and catching up."

"I see you found those journals. I've been looking everywhere for them, along with the photos. I think I've spent the better part of two or three weeks trying to find them."

"Why were you looking for these?"

"Oh, well, they were left for me," Jessica said. "It was one of the last things Patricia gave me before she passed. She knew I wanted to hold on to the memories we shared."

She hesitated before replying or handing over the journals. Rachel remembered the entry she had read from the first journal, so she knew Patricia hadn't put any information in them that could be used in the woman's favor. If there was something her grandmother wanted to hide, she would have kept it in the crypt. That much she knew after Mary had told her the woman had hidden the key. There was no other reason to hide the only way into the crypt unless she was trying to keep something away from the others.

Understanding by his body language that Josh wasn't comfortable with Jessica's demanding that she hand over the journals and photos, she didn't know what else she could do. There was no way she could argue against it, and more than anything, Rachel just wanted Jessica to go. The only way that was going to happen was to hand over everything they had just found. She had what she was looking for safely tucked into her bra.

Rachel slowly gathered everything into one pile and stood up. Jessica was nearly gloating as she reached out and took them from her, but she didn't leave right away. Jessica took a moment and quickly looked through the photos, glancing for a second at the journals in her other hand.

"I can't believe you found them without even trying," Jessica said. "Where were they? Was there anything else you found?"

"I don't think I'm comfortable sharing that information."

For a moment, it looked like the woman wanted to say something, but she didn't. Jessica glared at her a second longer before turning around and storming off. She had gotten what she wanted, and Rachel didn't understand the hostility. Still, she turned around and saw Josh was staring at her with a puzzled look on his face.

"What in the world was that all about?" he asked. "I mean, you said things were weird with her, but I wasn't expecting her to act so hostile about everything."

"I told you she came to me and said she was going

to move out and live in town until she could find another place, right?"

"Yeah. You also said she could stay here and you had no problem with letting her do that. That's why Grace is still here."

Rachel sighed. "Exactly. The thing is, when I came upstairs to go to my room, I heard something in here. When I opened the door, she was snooping around and acting sketchy when I came in. I think she's hiding something other than where she came from."

"I mean, I'm not going to tell you you're wrong if that's what you're looking for." Josh smiled. "That gut of yours has always been spot on when it comes to that stuff. With that in mind, if you think she's hiding something, you should trust it."

"Thank you for that. I'm really glad you came and that you support me. I really don't know what I'd do right now if you weren't here."

"Of course, I support you. Though I have to ask why you kept the key from her."

"After everything Mary explained to us today, I'm pretty sure this is the key that opens the crypt. I don't think Patricia was hiding anything in those journals, but I'm sure there is something in the crypt that she wanted to keep a secret."

"Like what?" he asked.

"I don't know, but after how Jessica has been acting about it all, I'd rather not let her know I have it. For all I know, she's the one my grandmother was keeping something from."

"We have dinner with your sister and Grace, but after that, I think we should go over there and see what we can find. At least by then, we'll know for sure the psycho is gone, and we won't have to worry about her following us."

"I like the idea of going there with you but not the dinner."

"What do you mean? I thought you had a good relationship with Grace."

"I wouldn't go that far. I just said she's not like her mother, but I don't know how to be sure about that. For now, I'm just going to play nice."

He nodded, and the two walked out of the library together. She didn't know how to admit to Josh that she was getting jealous of the attention he was getting from Grace, but she was hoping it would pass. As soon as they stepped out of the library and started to head downstairs, Rachel could hear the girls laughing and carrying on. It made her happy to know her sister was getting along with the other woman, even if she wasn't sure what kind of person she was yet. Suddenly, she heard a man's voice as well, and she paused.

It sounded familiar, though she couldn't quite place it until they made it to the main floor. Her sister and Grace were standing there, talking to Zach, and they all smiled when the couple walked into the parlor.

Even though he was wearing a grin on his face, Rachel could tell Zach was put off by the looks of Josh. He wasn't the average type of man from the area, but he was well-built and stood alone when it came to other men she had dated in the past. Josh didn't seem to notice and walked up to Zach and introduced himself. All she could do was smile at the way Zach was shocked by the approach, but he offered his hand in return.

"I'm Zach. It's nice to meet you, Josh."

"Nice to meet you, too."

"I already told Zach he was invited to dinner, too," Becky said. "So, it's going to be five of us instead of four."

Rachel nodded in acknowledgment, but she wasn't ready to spend so much time with the group. There was jealousy in the way Zach approached her boyfriend, and it was off-putting. She was dealing with her own jealousy, and she didn't want to put up with someone else's. Zach had no chance of getting to her, and Josh wanted no kind of intimate relationship with her sister. The whole thing was just getting to her in a way that she didn't know how to handle.

Still, she knew she needed to get away to catch her breath. She excused herself and explained she needed a minute alone. Josh tried to tag along, but she shot him down and told him she would only be a few minutes. Zach was trying to get close to both sisters, and Rachel didn't like the way he was doing it. However, Becky was getting along with everyone. Something had to give.

She quickly made her way out of the room and headed down the hallway. Having Josh there was something she was glad had happened, but everything that came along with it was too much. She couldn't handle the way Grace kept looking at him, and now Zach was judging him, too. Rachel sighed and continued toward the front door, thankful for a moment of peace.

26

The walk across the property was already starting to clear her mind. She still didn't have the answers she really wanted, but at least she wasn't surrounded by so many people. Sometimes, just some fresh air would help her to refocus.

Rachel hated the idea of being in the middle of drama. Although a large part of what she was dealing with now was exactly that, it was somehow different. There were so many things going on around her, and she had no way of knowing what was going on. Jessica's lying about things and then finding out the truth about her mother's death. Plus, the idea of their grandmother knowing about them and never coming to find them. All she wanted to do was learn the truth about what actually had happened all those years ago.

As the minutes continued to pass, she was thankful to have the view in front of her. The tall green grass tickled her fingertips while she looked up at the clear sky. The warm air felt good in her lungs with every breath she took. Rachel found herself thinking about the time her mother had stayed at the estate with Patricia. It took her back to wondering why Patricia had never come for them. There was nothing stopping her from bringing them to their rightful place.

There was a resentment for the woman that she couldn't explain. Though a part of her knew she had every right to be angry that she had never come, there was no explanation as to why. She couldn't blame the woman without fully understanding why she had chosen to do the things she did. Without realizing how far she had walked or how long she was gone, Rachel found herself wandering around to the back porch and standing on the steps.

The glowing rays of sunshine were starting to fade away as the sun was starting to set. It was one of the most magnificent views she had ever seen, and she closed her eyes to soak in the last bit of warmth from the evening light. As the world around them started to darken into nightfall, Rachel couldn't take her mind off the crypt.

It was calling to her, begging to be explored. Though she had made a promise to Josh that the two would check it out together, there was something in there that she needed to see. It continued to call to her as she looked off at the sunset. She really wanted to keep that promise and search the crypt with Josh, but she couldn't control the urge to move. It was like something was pulling her toward it, and

Rachel reached into her pocket and pulled out the key.

Feeling the weight of it in her hand, she knew it held all the answers she was looking for. Whatever Jessica wanted was in there, along with whatever her grandmother had tried to hide from the world. Before she even knew it, she was moving. Rachel stood up from the steps and started walking in the direction of the crypt. She needed to go, and there wasn't anything keeping her from doing it right then. Though the trance-like state she was in gave her no control over her body.

In her mind, she was merely taking a walk and thinking about what could be inside, but the reality was that she was nearing the gate to the cemetery. Before she could understand what was happening to her, Rachel was walking by the headstones and toward the entryway to the crypt. It was the third time she had visited the cemetery, but it was the first time she had heard the sound of rushing water in the distance. From the story she had heard from Mary, she knew the Red River was nearby.

As she looked in the direction from where she heard the water, there was a narrow path covered in foliage. It was easy to see why they hadn't noticed it on their first trip to the cemetery, and Rachel was fascinated with it. It was slightly hidden by the overgrowth of shrubs and grass and hidden right next to the cemetery. With each passing moment, the sun fell lower from the sky and left a red haze throughout the property. The soft glow on the path gave her a peculiar sensation, like something was waiting for her on the other side.

Just like the crypt had called to her moments before, the path was doing the same. Without hesitation, she let her feet guide her way, and a second later, she was walking down the path. Even the overgrown plant life couldn't stop her from moving toward the river. The pull from the current that she wasn't even in seemed to keep her from stopping. There was something in the way it called to her that made her want to go. Rachel didn't even know where she was going until there was a voice hollering out her name.

At first, Rachel thought it was coming from the other side of the path she was on. A moment later, she heard it again, and it stopped her in her tracks. The person calling her name was coming from the yard behind her, and she shook off the trance before realizing she wasn't on the back porch. The entire thing had left her confused and wondering how she had gotten there. Instead of being by the house where she thought she had been, she was a few feet away from the swampy forest and everything that lay beyond it.

The third time she heard her name being called, she knew it was Josh. Everything inside of her wanted to turn back around and run to him, but she couldn't move. When Rachel tried to speak, nothing came out. She tried over and over to call the man she loved. Yet there was nothing she could do to stop herself from moving forward. The pull was stronger than she could manage, and she found that no matter how hard she tried to scream out, the words wouldn't come out.

As the sound of the rushing water became closer, Rachel knew the path was taking her directly to the river's edge. She was terrified of what was coming, and the splashing sounds of water beating against the rocks only intensified the feeling of fear washing over her. She tried everything to move under her own power, but none of it was of any use as the water quickly came into view. Seeing it for the first time caused her heart to race. The view was more intense than the sound could have ever been.

The water was just a few feet in front of her, and the soles of her shoes were touching the edge. Something inside of her made her start to take the next step, and Rachel couldn't do anything to stop it. It was almost like someone else was controlling her movement. Her heart started pounding faster and faster. The lump in her throat grew. She couldn't breathe, and even when she tried, she couldn't scream. Just before her foot touched the top of the water, something grabbed hold of her and pulled her back. Instantly, the trance was broken.

Stumbling backward and away from the river, Rachel fell to the ground but landed in Josh's waiting arms. She was still trembling with fear as she tried to regain control of herself. A small part of her only knew what was happening toward the end of the trance, but even then, she couldn't stop herself from walking into the river. She was trying to catch her breath when Josh spoke to her with panic in his voice.

"What in the hell happened? I was calling for you, but you just kept walking away from me."

"I don't know if I can explain what happened. It was like I was being pulled in this direction or pushed. I really don't know."

Josh scoffed. "After what you just put me through, I think you better at least try to tell me what's going on."

"I can try," Rachel said. "See, when I came out here and found my mother's headstone, I had been following a spirit. She led me to the marker before disappearing."

Josh only nodded, but he was giving her his full attention as she went on in detail about a couple of times she had seen the spirit and the way the crypt called for her. She even told him how she had no control over herself as she walked to the river's edge. As Rachel explained the dreams she was having and how she thought they were in connection to how her mother had died, he wrapped his arms around her.

"We should get you back to the house," Josh said.

"I-I think that's a good idea," Rachel muttered.

He held her tightly as they walked to the manor through the yard. No matter how much better having him there was making her feel, she knew something was wrong. Either someone or something was evil at the estate.

27

The couple had made it back to her bedroom and were sitting on the edge of her bed. Rachel was still shaken to the core, but having Josh by her side and holding her tightly was starting to make a world of difference. After everything she had been through in just the few days they had been at the estate, she felt like she was left with more questions than answers.

"I have something for you," Josh said.

"What is it?"

Josh smiled. "It's just a little necklace. I figured it would come in handy for the key. That way, you can never lose it, and it will always be with you."

As he reached into his pocket and pulled out a gold chain, she couldn't help but be touched by the notion that he was constantly thinking about her. The man was truly everything one could ask for in a partner, and she blushed as he took the key from her hand, placed the necklace through it, and wrapped it around her neck. It felt amazing to have Josh back in her life, no matter how long they had been apart.

"You know, we still have a little time before dinner," Rachel said.

Josh grinned. "What do you have in mind?"

"Nothing that's going through your mind, though maybe sometime later. I was thinking about the first journal I found, and I'd really like to read a little more of it."

"That's what I was thinking about, too. You're so dirty minded. I'm a gentleman, and here you are trying to get me in bed. Filthy animal."

Rachel laughed and pulled out the journal. The two spent the next twenty minutes reading entry after entry. None of what they read went into much detail about what they were looking for, but it was still nice to learn more about her grandmother.

"I'm surprised Patricia liked dogs that much. If you look around the property, there's no sign that there had ever been a dog or cat."

"Well, she was getting older, so I guess it's possible it had been a few years since the last time she had one," Rachel replied.

Josh smiled. "You're probably right, but even after she stopped raising them, she still donated a lot of money to the local charity drives and animal rescues. I feel like you have a lot in common with the woman."

"I do love animals, but I don't think I like them as much as she did."

"Well, she loved her daughter even more from the looks of it."

Rachel chuckled. "From what I can tell, she adored Amanda. I don't think there is anything that she wouldn't have done for our mother."

As she went back to reading the entries, Rachel came across the name Collin Hunter. He had been mentioned several times, and Patricia spoke of the man with a fondness that made her feel as though they had been close. Patricia didn't mention many names, but his was within the pages many times. There was a love there that couldn't be explained other than how he looked after the woman and gave her a solid foundation.

Collin had come into Patricia's and Amanda's life not long after Amanda turned sixteen. She kept reading and was touched when she realized he had been like a father to Amanda at a time when she needed one the most. The teenage years were the most prolific in a young woman's life, and it was nice to see she had that kind of person in her life. On the other hand, Collin had kept things proper with Patricia. He was nothing more than a confidante and close friend to her grandmother.

"I wonder what happened to Collin. No one has mentioned his name since we've been here," Rachel muttered out loud.

She continued to try to read the next entry, but she noticed Josh had taken out his phone and was typing away. It made it hard to concentrate on the journal, so she waited for him to finish, wondering what could have been so important. A moment later, he chuckled and looked up at her.

"What is it?"

"It looks as though Collin Hunter is still alive, and he actually lives in the area. From what I found on the internet, he owns a few factories and a property about ten miles from here."

Rachel smiled. "Well, I think that's the best lead I've had since getting here. How do you feel about paying the man a visit?"

"I'm all about hunting down the answers you're looking for, but we do have dinner with everyone here shortly. I'm sure it's about done now, actually."

Instantly, she was disappointed. More than anything else, Rachel wanted to talk to the man Patricia had written so fondly about. Still, she knew they could wait until the next day to see Collin. They had already made a commitment when they agreed to the dinner, and they needed to keep up appearances.

Rachel didn't know how the dinner was going to work, with everyone acting the way they had earlier. The one thing she knew for sure was that if things got too bad, she'd be heading to her room for an early night. Josh smiled at her and stood up. Suddenly, she dreaded the idea of going to dinner. There was something about the man she loved smiling at her that made her not want to leave the room. She begrudgingly stood up with him, and the two headed downstairs to the dining room.

The moment they walked in and she saw Zach

sitting beside her sister, Rachel wanted to scream. Though he had come off initially as a nice guy, she didn't like the way he was setting his sights on Becky. Even if she hadn't been thrilled that the man was joining them for dinner, Becky looked like she was in love with the attention he was giving her. In that aspect of things, Rachel was happy for her, but when she turned to greet Grace, she could tell she wasn't as joyful as the other two.

Rachel looked at her boyfriend, who seemed to notice the same thing she had. Josh gave her a looked that she understood, and she nodded back her approval of what he was asking her. Along with the nod, she was giving him her approval to focus his attention on Grace. The girl was sweet, and no matter how she felt about things going on around them, she didn't deserve to sit around and see her former fling making moves on someone new. In her eyes, no one did.

It wasn't something she would normally do for anyone, but one look at the girl and anyone could tell she was full of jealousy mixed with sadness. Rachel didn't want to see Grace upset when they were just trying to all get along. Josh took the seat next to Grace but next to Rachel as well. Her own jealousy needed to take a back seat to the current situation. In her heart, she knew Josh only had eyes for her.

Throughout dinner, they all drank alcohol. Rachel was thankful for the continuous pouring of wine and whatever else she had been drinking. It helped keep everyone on a level playing field, and Josh keeping his attention more on Grace helped the evening move forward without disaster following. It was only when Becky offered to walk Zach back to his car that she could see the wounded expression on Grace's face. She had been in the woman's shoes before, though not in a very long time. It wasn't anything she wanted to see someone else go through.

Without thinking about it a moment longer, she nudged Josh's arm when Grace was looking down. He gave her a knowing look and cleared his throat. While Rachel was perfectly comfortable spending a little more time with Grace, she wasn't about to let the two spend any time together alone.

"Grace, why don't you join us in the parlor for one more nightcap?" Josh said. "I think we've drunk enough to hold off a small army, but it never hurts to have one more."

She smiled. "I think I'd like that, Josh."

While Rachel didn't like the underlying tone in her voice, she knew Josh was quite the catch and couldn't blame the girl for laying it on thick. Still, she was glad her boyfriend had mentioned that both of them would be with her. She didn't want Grace to feel like she couldn't be trusted, even if that was what the jealousy in her heart was saying. She knew the only reason she was so agreeable was that she was looking forward to visiting the crypt. Otherwise, she probably wouldn't have let Josh invite the girl to a nightcap.

28

Rachel followed Josh and Grace. She was thankful she'd taken the time earlier in the tour to pour them both a drink. Now, Josh knew exactly where everything was and quickly readied a round of drinks for the trio. As they sat back and continued on the conversation from dinner, she kept a close watch on the front door. Her sister had been outside now for ten minutes. Every time the ancient house creaked, she jumped in anticipation of seeing Becky walk through the door.

Josh, bless his heart, did everything in his power to keep the conversation going and keep them all distracted. As they finished their drinks, though, it became apparent they were going to need more than one to get Grace into her room. Instead of letting Josh make the next round, Rachel quickly volunteered. She took the opportunity to pass by the massive bay windows and peek outside. Her sister was in Zach's arms, kissing him passionately on the hood of the man's car.

Rolling her eyes, she tried not to let her emotions convey through her expression. There was no reason to upset Grace more. She and Becky were going to have to have a conversation later, though, about proper etiquette when dating a friend's ex. Sitting back down, she turned her attention back to the others as Rachel handed out the drinks.

"So, Josh, is your life on the road incredibly interesting?" Grace asked.

He chuckled and shook his head. "The only time I really enjoy it is when I have layovers like this where I can come to see my girl."

Grace pouted. "That must be hard, always being apart. I don't think I could ever be away from someone for so long. No, I'd be the type of girlfriend who would come with you…hypothetically."

Rachel rolled her eyes, shooting her partner an apologetic look. The young woman was quickly on her way to being completely plastered. Still, she wasn't sure how much more of the blatant attempts at flirting with Rachel's boyfriend she could take.

She had positioned herself in the parlor so she could see the hallway leading to the front door. Rachel was glad she had made the decision when she spotted her sister coming back through the front door and start heading in their direction. After everything that had transpired up to that point, she wanted to make sure there wasn't any more stress on Grace. When Becky looked up, it was easy to see that her cheeks were flushed and something had gone on between her and Zach before she made her way back inside.

Rachel quickly shook her head and indicated that Becky's coming to join them was a very bad idea. She quickly grew disappointed, but Becky gave her sister a look of understanding and turned around. She hated that she had to do things that way, but there wasn't another way to keep the evening from ending in fireworks. Glancing over at her guest, she knew Grace had heard her sister come in.

"I think this is a good time to head to bed for the night," Rachel said.

Grace scoffed. "Come on, we were just getting this party started."

"There will be plenty of time for all of us to party on a different night," Josh replied. "I think we've done enough damage for one evening."

She quickly nodded and tried to stand up. It didn't take much for her and Josh to realize the girl wouldn't be making it to bed on her own, and they each grabbed an arm and helped her down the hallway, up the stairs, and into her room. Grace couldn't hold her alcohol, but she still managed to do better than most people Rachel had seen over the years. As they helped her to bed, the couple smiled at each other. They had somehow managed to keep the night from falling apart and kept Grace in good spirits as well.

When the pair finally made it back into Rachel's bedroom, they were exhausted and beyond tipsy. She hated the idea of the crypt going undisturbed one more night but knew they were in no state to make the trek down to the cemetery to see what her grandmother had left behind. It was locked away and safe. Climbing into bed next to the man she loved, there was nothing else she wanted to think about beyond the joy that she felt with Josh there. It wasn't long before they drifted off to sleep.

RACHEL WOKE FEELING GROGGY. The inklings of a hangover had already started to etch their way into her head. Her hands searched for Josh but came up empty, the bed cold where he should have been sleeping. Forcing her eyes open, Rachel saw that it was still night outside. The sun hadn't started its trip yet across the sunrise.

"Josh?" she called out.

Immediately, Rachel looked around, her eyes adjusting to the dark. There was no light coming from the adjacent bathroom, but she still rose and went to the door, knocking softly but getting no reply. Grabbing her robe from the end of the bed, Rachel crept to the bedroom door and cracked it open. The hallway's dim lighting stung her eyes, a rush of cold air sending a chill down her spine. Somewhere in the back of her mind, it registered that the house had no air conditioning, and it was a balmy seventy-five degrees outside.

There was a faint glow emanating from beneath

the door of the library. Rachel clutched the key that dangled around her neck, its presence there reassuring her that no one had robbed her in her sleep. Moving slowly, she reached for the knob and carefully opened the door. Her heart started to race as the light flooded the hallway. She distinctly remembered turning off the lights when they'd last left, but that didn't mean someone hadn't enjoyed the hundreds of books since that time.

What made her heart race, though, was the opened office door inside the library. No one was supposed to know about the secret room, not beyond Becky and herself. She closed the library door behind her, not wanting the others to see. Whispering for Josh once again and getting no reply, Rachel moved closer to the small space hidden within the walls. Josh had no reason to be in the office without her. Right away, she was on edge.

Still, even if it wasn't Josh within the hidden space, Rachel thought for sure she was hearing someone moving around on the other side. Trying to catch whoever it was off guard, she quickly dashed around the corner and entered the office, but no one was inside. What had she been hearing if there wasn't anyone there?

A sudden chill moved through her when she thought about the noise she had followed. There wasn't anyone in the room, but a moment before, it was clear to her that someone had been there. Suddenly, she started to panic as she realized the door behind her was starting to close. Rachel spun around and tried to stop it, knowing the small space wasn't enough for her to get out. A moment later, the door was closed, and she was trapped inside.

Though it hadn't been much of a problem before, she quickly found herself becoming claustrophobic. The walls inside the little room felt as though they were moving in all around her. Rachel's heart started to beat faster, and she was having a hard time breathing. Clutching the key around her neck, she tried to calm herself down.

"It's just a room. Someone will come to find you. Becky and Josh both know about the room, so they'll come looking for you. It's all going to be okay," she whispered to herself.

Rachel pictured all the beautiful things in her life and tried to focus on them. The estate, her sister, and Josh. Josh, the man she loved more than anything else. Her sister would follow her anywhere just so they could be together. The estate, where she was learning all about her grandmother and, hopefully, her mother, too.

With her hand still wrapped around the key, Rachel forced herself to calm down. Moving her hand along the wall, she found the switch for the lights and flicked them on, but nothing happened. Cursing herself for not bringing her phone along for the midnight walk, Rachel did her best to use her now-throbbing brain to work through the situation. There had to be a lighter, match, or even a lamp in the room. Perhaps even an escape hatch.

Her fingers moved along the smooth surface of

the wall until, at last, she found something of interest. It was a small crevice but one that held inherent familiarity. A keyhole. She quickly pulled off the necklace, feeling her way back down to the opening and saying a silent prayer as she stuck the key into the hole. Relief coursed through her when it clicked open.

29

There was something about the sound of the door opening that sent waves of relief coursing through Rachel. She had never thought much about her dislike for enclosed spaces before. After all, most of her adult life had been spent living in a camper with her sister. It was different when you had open air and windows all around you. The dark cavern of the office was enough to make anyone slightly nauseous. It was nice knowing the key worked on the hidden door. With the relief still working its way through her body, Rachel pushed open the door and stepped into the library.

The light was off now, a sickening feeling moving through her. Someone had to have been waiting for her to step into the office. Rachel didn't hesitate as she moved for the door, making her way back into her bedroom, where she flipped on the lights. Josh bolted upright in bed, obviously rousing from a deep sleep. She had known him for long enough to recognize when her boyfriend had been out cold for some time. The room was warm with the humid Alabama night. Nothing was making sense anymore. Josh was on his feet and at her side before she made it to the bed.

"Hey, are you okay?" Josh asked.

"Where did you go?" Rachel whispered.

"What do you mean, sweetheart? I haven't left the bed since we crashed like…six hours ago. What's going on, honey? Did something happen?"

She shook her head, unable to answer him. How could she explain that they were under attack from an unseen force? That the people they lived with might be monsters? There was no way that she was going to be able to get back to sleep. Josh wrapped his arms around her. His mere presence was all she needed for the anxiety to start to wane.

"I woke up a little while ago, and you weren't in bed. I don't know where you went, but you definitely weren't lying beside me," Rachel said.

"I was right here the entire time. I haven't even gotten up to get a drink of water or use the bathroom."

"Still, you were gone when I woke up. So, I went to the library to see if maybe you were in there, but when I got there, the door to the secret room was open. I didn't see why you would have been in there, so I tried to catch whoever it was when they closed the door on me, and I was trapped inside."

"I'm sorry, but I'm a light sleeper, and I didn't hear anything. As far as I know, I've never been one to sleepwalk, either."

Rachel sighed. "I don't know what happened. I woke up, and you were gone. I just…I can't explain it, Josh, but you were gone."

"I promise you, sweetheart. I haven't gone anywhere all night. I've been right here."

"I believe you, but I swear I saw it differently. Then, when I was trapped inside, I started to freak out. When I found the switch inside to open the door, the light in the library was off, just like someone had been in there and shut me in on purpose."

Josh shrugged. "I'm glad you were able to get out, but I never went into the library for anything. Only earlier when you took me there."

"I don't understand what happened then. I know when I first woke up, I was really cold. Almost to the point that I was shivering."

Josh cocked his head, giving her a confused look before reaching across the bed to grab his phone. He pulled up the thermostat and showed her that it was well over seventy degrees. It was strange, but Rachel knew something supernatural was happening. Forcing herself to think back to when the temperature changed, she gasped.

'I don't think you got up last night at all," Rachel said. "I think it was another weird dream, but this time, I was sleepwalking. When I got back out of the office, the door was closed, and the light was off, but it was warm—not like when I first woke up."

The look of concern in her partner's eyes stirred the protective nature inside of her. She hated that he was worried, but she knew he wasn't questioning her sanity. The house was definitely haunted, and that was something they both took seriously. It was another game altogether if the entity was able to take control of a living being and make them see things that weren't there. She hated that she was getting the brunt of the spirit's force, but at the same time, she was grateful it wasn't happening to Grace or Becky. At least Rachel knew what she was up against.

Her body started to tremble as the adrenaline fizzled out, and she was left with the aftermath of the panic attack. They had to figure out what was going on there. The spirit was her mother. She was certain of that, but why was it trying to take her into the water? Away from the house? Why had it tried to trap her in the office? There was more going on, and Rachel was determined to find out what that was. With the key clutched in her hand, she tried to sort through her thoughts. They were coming at her like bullets, but her fatigued and hung-over mind was struggling to process anything.

"I believe everything you're telling me, Rachel. I've never had any reason not to. I do think, however, it might be time to call in a professional to see what's really going on around here," Josh said.

"What do you mean?"

"Well, I know there are some mediums who can

talk to spirits. Maybe we should give one a call and have them come to the estate."

Rachel groaned. "Why didn't I think of that?"

"You've been going through a lot as it is. No reason to beat yourself up. I just happened to think of it first."

"I'm really glad you're here. We'll find one tomorrow and put in a call. I want to know what's going on around here."

Josh smiled. "We'll figure it out, honey. Now, try to get some sleep."

She was completely exhausted from the day before and having been woken up sometime during the night. Rachel tried to lay in bed and close her eyes, but she kept tossing and turning for several minutes before Josh sat up and put his hand on her leg.

"Maybe going to sleep isn't going to work out right away, but I know something that might help."

"Yeah? What's that?"

"How about I draw you a nice warm bath? Maybe that will help you relax enough to get to sleep."

Rachel grinned. "I think that might be the most perfect thing you've ever said. You know me too well."

"No such thing."

He jumped out of bed and entered the attached bathroom. A moment later, Rachel could hear the water running. She quickly took off her necklace and tried to think of a good place to hide it. An old trick she had learned while traveling was to hide things under the lining of her boot. She'd done it with cash for years and knew it would work for the necklace. Josh called out to her that the bath was ready, and she smiled.

Standing up, she untied the robe but paused when she felt someone else's presence in the room. Wrapping the robe back around her body, Rachel slowly turned, her heart racing at the sight of her mother's spirit standing near the window. She wanted to call out for Josh, for him to see the entity firsthand, but at the same time, Rachel didn't want to risk scaring the spirit away. Moving with intentional caution, she moved to stand next to the creature at the window. It was a terrifying and bewildering sensation. A chilling air seemed to emit from the creature. Rachel didn't know what to say to the woman or if she could hear her daughter at all.

"I wanted to bring you here. I wanted you and your sister to know your grandmother and how wonderful the estate could be," she whispered.

"Why did you leave us?" Rachel asked.

"It wasn't safe for you here. It's still not. You need to take your loved ones and go…before it's too late."

"What do you mean, too late? Is someone after us? Is it Jessica?"

"I don't have the answers you're looking for, sweet child. Go now, leave here—"

"Not until I know what happened, why you abandoned us, why you left us behind," Rachel hissed.

She watched in stunned horror as the spirit started to dissipate before her very eyes. There was nothing she could do, despite calling out for her mother. Just as the creature evaporated, Josh came barreling into the room, ready to defend her against any danger. As she softly started to cry, he held her, knowing it was all he could do.

30

After taking a long bath, she was able to fall asleep quickly in her boyfriend's arms. By the time she woke, it was well after ten in the morning. Rachel bolted upright, finding the bed empty but knowing it wasn't another hallucination from the humid air passing through the room from the two opened windows. The wonderful man had left her a note on the nightstand next to her phone. She smiled when she read it.

You looked like you needed some sleep—I didn't want to wake you. I'm headed to town for some breakfast. Why don't you join me downstairs on the back porch when you're up and ready? I adore you—Josh.

Rachel wasted no time jumping from bed and getting dressed. At the prospect of breakfast and coffee, her stomach growled with anticipation. Ten minutes after waking up, she was pulling on her boots and jogging down to meet Josh. She left the key in her boot. It was a secure place that wouldn't flash its existence all over the community. Without knowing what kind of a man Collin Hunter was, she wasn't going to give away any information. Jogging down the steps and out the back door, she smiled when she saw Josh sitting and working on his laptop.

It brought her pleasure beyond words that he was there with them. When he heard her coming, he rose and greeted her with a tender embrace and kiss. Her heart raced at his every touch, but there would be time later to appreciate him in earnest. She sat down as Josh poured her a cup of coffee. He had found the bakery. The tabletop was littered with boxes of croissants, breakfast sandwiches, toast wedges, and cheese. She didn't hesitate to dive right into the feast. Josh chuckled with amusement as he closed his computer and turned his attention to her.

"I'm glad you finally were able to get up and join me."

"You're the one who didn't wake me before you left."

"I know, but you looked so peaceful that I didn't want to wake you. Between that and knowing you didn't sleep very well last night, I thought it was better to let you sleep."

Rachel smiled. "I never said I was complaining about it. I'm glad you let me sleep in. I actually feel well rested for the first time in days."

"I'm happy to hear it. Now, I've been doing a bunch of research about what we talked about last night. It looks like there are three psychic mediums in the area. Two of them didn't have the best reviews. I figured I'd run into a few of them that were probably just faking it for the money."

"Okay, so what about the third?"

"I thought you'd never ask," Josh replied. "The last one is well established and looks promising. Plenty of good reviews to go along with it, as well."

"So, I suppose we go with the one who has a chance of doing a good job. Have you had the chance to call the number?"

"I was actually waiting for you before I made the decision."

Rachel had a mouth full of food by the time he replied. Trying not to look like a pig in a pen, she tried to chew and swallow in one motion but ended up choking slightly, regardless. Josh just smiled at her and pretended not to see her struggling. She quickly finished chewing and swallowed the rest but took a drink before speaking.

"You're more than welcome to make the call. I'm happy enough just sitting here, stuffing my face with breakfast." She smiled.

"That works for me. I love watching you eat."

"Oh, yeah. It's so attractive," Rachel replied with another mouth full of food.

Before he could dial the number, the back door opened, and Becky appeared, looking as rough as Rachel had felt hours before. She looked beyond relieved when she saw the others sitting there with a plethora of coffee and food. Josh must have anticipated her joining them. He quickly produced another to-go cup full of coffee and set it in front of an empty chair. Becky plopped down, grabbing the cup and muttering "thank you" to Josh. Rachel couldn't pass up the opportunity to give her sister a hard time.

"Rough night?" Rachel asked.

Becky glared at her. "Funny. I swear I didn't drink that much, but I sure as hell feel like shit this morning."

"Yeah, I think we've all been there," Josh said. "So, what have you got on the roster for today, sis?"

Becky sighed. "Well, I planned on having breakfast with Zach but considering that was two hours ago…I'm pretty sure I've got a bridge to unburn."

The conversation reminded Rachel of the night before with Grace. She had to have a tough talk with her sister. No matter what the will stated, they were guests in a house that Grace had made her home. Becky flaunting her new romance around the poor girl wasn't doing anyone any favors. She wanted her sister to be happy, but she didn't want to stir the pot, either. They barely knew the locals, but Rachel had to presume they were loyal to Jessica and Grace, given their tenure in the area.

Despite how easygoing she was with Josh, Rachel didn't want to have it with him around. Thankfully, Josh knew her well, and one look was all it took for him to excuse himself, claiming a need to use the restroom. The ruse wasn't lost on Becky. She groaned and rolled her eyes in anticipation of the conversation to come.

"We need to have a talk," Rachel said.

"That doesn't sound good. I suppose I'm not going to like this, am I?"

"Probably not, but we still need to have it. I think you should slow things down with Zach. Just for now."

Becky scoffed. "Why would I need to do that? We're having a good time together, and it's not like we're hurting anyone. Besides, am I not allowed to be happy like you are with Josh?"

"Of course, you're allowed to be happy, but we just got here. I know he and Grace aren't together, but she has feelings, too. She's still hurting over losing him, and it's like a slap in the face every time the two of you get all flirty with each other in front of her."

"From what Zach has been telling me, she was quite the witch toward him when they were together. You don't understand how bad it got for him."

"What do you mean by that?" Rachel asked.

"It took him a little while to catch on, but he figured out she was only with him for his money. Once he stopped spending so much on her, her attitude changed completely."

"I wouldn't go taking sides until you know both sides of the story."

"I'm only going by what he said, but you don't know the facts like I do. Besides, Zach said I shouldn't even bring it up because you would say something like that. Maybe you're the one who should do some digging before you tell me what to believe."

Before Rachel could take the conversation any further, her sister sighed and stood up.

"Listen, I don't want to fight with you, okay?" Becky said. "I'm tired and hungover, worse than I've ever been before. Can we just talk about this later?"

Rachel nodded but didn't say anything. Becky turned and headed back into the house just as Josh emerged. He gave Rachel a look as he sat down. She sighed and quickly told him everything that had been said. There was nothing they could do about the situation beyond exactly what Zach suggested through Becky. If any of them had something to hide, Rachel was going to find out with Josh's help. Turning their attention back to the problem at hand, she listened as Josh called the medium he'd picked and set up an appointment for later that evening.

There was no hiding the hitch in the woman's voice when Josh had shared the address of the estate. Still, Rachel was going to take it as a good sign that the psychic hadn't immediately canceled the session. Rachel was hopeful the woman, if nothing else, might be able to share some of her knowledge of the estate with them. If they had time, Rachel wanted to invite Mary to the séance later that evening. With the first of many tasks knocked out and the reward being the crypt later in the day, the pair cleaned up their breakfast mess and prepared to head out for the morning. She was anxious to meet with Collin Hunter and find out what the man knew about her family's sordid history.

31

"Have you ever seen anything so beautiful before?" Rachel asked.

Josh shook his head. "No, and I've been all across this country. Out here, though, it feels like time is standing still."

"I couldn't agree more. It makes me never want to leave."

He cocked his head as they drove. She knew the statement was a rare one for her to make, but it was the God's honest truth. The estate was the first place where she truly felt like she was at home. There was still something wrong at the manor, but that wasn't going to deter her from finding out what was going on and what had happened to her mother and grandmother. The lingering questions ate away at her.

"Really?"

Rachel nodded. "I don't know what it is about the place, but it really feels like home. I'm sure it's just because my mother and grandmother were there... maybe that will pass."

"But maybe not. I guess I'd never really thought about you calling any place your home for longer than a few months at the most," Josh said.

"And that's still liable to happen, but right now, I want to know who my family was, you know?"

He nodded in understanding. She adored that she could talk to him about anything, yet he never pressured her to have conversations that Rachel wasn't ready for. It was a mutual love and respect that they shared. In time, she might be able to explain what it was about the estate, but until then, the answer would have to wait. As the address in question came into view, Rachel's heart started to race. Parked in the driveway was a familiar car from the night before. Josh brought his pickup to a halt behind Zach's petite sports car just as the man stepped out of the large ranch house. The couple climbed out of the truck. Zach looked shocked and slightly aggravated to see the pair as he approached them.

"What are the two of you doing here?" Zach asked.

"We heard Collin was a close friend of the family, and after doing a little research, we were able to figure out he was still in the area," Rachel said. "I just wanted to meet the man and maybe talk to him a little about my grandmother."

Zach seemed to just stand in front of them, dumbfounded. She didn't understand why he suddenly had changed the way he acted toward her.

As she tried to read his expression, she remembered her sister was supposed to meet with him for breakfast and had overslept. She brushed off the way he was acting as him being upset about that. Though she was curious about what he was doing at Collin's house.

"Well, that's neither here nor there. He's an elderly man these days, and he doesn't take too kindly to visitors. Collin likes to keep to himself mostly and doesn't like to be disturbed."

Rachel smiled. "That's okay. I don't blame him for not wanting any visitors, but I promise it will only take a few minutes. I'm only curious about the man who used to be so close to my grandmother."

"I still don't think it's a good idea. I'll tell him you stopped by, but seeing him isn't going to—"

Suddenly, his phone rang, and Zach excused himself from the couple. Rachel didn't understand what he was doing there in the first place, and she knew he had ignored her question on purpose. Still, watching him step away to talk on the phone, she could tell he was adamant they didn't meet Collin. She was starting to wonder if this was going to be another secret that she was going to have to uncover.

Rachel turned her attention to Josh. He looked like he was ready to hit the smug man, but she knew he'd keep himself cool and collected. Josh was a proud man, turning to self-control until the violence was absolutely necessary to protect himself or someone else. She appreciated that he was as irritated as she was. Seconds later, the man was back, his irritated expression the same but now with flushed cheeks. She took some amusement in knowing that whatever call he'd taken had ruffled his proper feathers a little.

"I don't know if you are here because of some bidding of Grace's, but I assure you, that woman is not what she seems," Zach hissed.

"That's what I keep hearing, but my opinion of her is of no concern to you. We are here to speak to an old friend of my grandmother, that's all," she said.

"Well, I can't stop you, but you should know his mind is slipping. Anything he has to offer you will be nothing more than the ramblings of an old lunatic. Patricia tried for years to get him some help, but he's hellbent on staying here."

"Is that why you are here? To help him?" she asked.

The look in the man's gaze softened as he nodded. For the first time, she found herself wondering if she'd approached Zach all wrong. Rachel despised the fact that the estate warped her sense of right and wrong when it came to people. Normally, her empath abilities were spot on when it came to deciphering who someone was deep down. Grace had been nothing but kind, if not a bit stand-offish at first. Perhaps there was more to her than Rachel realized. She had to give everyone a fair chance, including Zach, if not for herself, then for Becky.

"Patricia cared a great deal about Collin. I never quite understood why, but she did make me promise to check in on the old man from time to time when she passed. So, out of respect for your grandmother, I stop by and keep an eye on him the best I can."

"Honestly, I never realized you were that close to my grandmother," Rachel said. "Of course, this is the first time we've actually had a real conversation about anything."

"I really didn't even know who she was until the first few times I came to pick Grace up to go out," Zach said. "By the third time I was there and waiting for her to get ready, Victoria and I were hitting it off fairly well. Sometimes, Grace would take hours getting ready, or every once in a while, she'd stand me up altogether."

"So, you got to spend a lot of time with Patricia?"

"On the days Grace would stand me up, I'd get to spend most of the evening with her. The woman was full of old stories, and I loved listening to her talk."

Rachel sighed. "I should apologize to you for snapping at you. It's been a long few days, and I never should have taken it out on you."

"I appreciate that. I won't hold it against you, but I do need to be on my way. I have a meeting in town soon that I just can't afford to miss."

"Well, thank you for your time, Zach. I'm sure we'll see you around."

"I certainly hope so," he smiled.

The couple watched him pull away, but Rachel was still conflicted about the situation. The picture he painted of Grace was nothing like the young woman she was getting to know back at the estate. It was spinning the web in her mind even deeper into oblivion. Josh squeezed her hand, pulling her attention back to the current situation. She had to keep her head in the game and was thankful her partner was there to remind her of that.

"Are you okay? We can always head back and call today a wash if you want," Josh said.

She shook her head. "No. If Collin Hunter knew my grandmother and mother, then I want to talk with him. He might be the only connection we have left. Mary knew them, but she wasn't around when they had their falling out or when my mother returned before she…before she died. It has to be Collin."

"All right, honey, I'm on board all the way. I just wanted you to be sure," Josh said.

She leaned on the tips of her toes and kissed the man's cheek before they headed for the front door. Her heart was pounding with anticipation. Whatever they learned on the other side, Rachel knew it would bring them one step closer to unraveling the mystery of Red River. Josh gave her one final wink of support before he knocked on the door. They waited with bated breath for it to open. As the seconds passed and her heart raced, Rachel wondered if the man was going to answer. She didn't have to ponder for long.

32

The irritated man standing in front of them was nothing like she'd expected. From Zach's description, Rachel had envisioned a decrepit elderly man, yet Collin Hunter towered over her. Only the silver of his hair and protruding stomach seemed to age him. The color drained from his face when he saw Rachel standing there, making her wonder if it was his mother's ghost that he saw in her eyes.

"You're the daughter, right? Ain't there supposed to be two of you?" he asked.

Rachel nodded as she cleared her throat. "My name is Rachel Groves, and this is my boyfriend, Josh. I was wondering if you had a few minutes to talk with us?"

He gave her a curt bow, stepping aside to let the pair into his house. Despite the modest size of the house, it was lavishly decorated. Obviously, the man had some wealth to his name. It was starting to make sense how he knew her family. They had stumbled into the world of the wealthy the instant she and Becky had been named inheritors of the estate. Everything was different now. Collin led the pair into a living room, motioning for them to sit on a leather sofa as he sat across from them in a recliner.

Collin was still looking at her with a peculiar gaze that she couldn't quite make out. Whatever it was, it was making her gut churn with enough trepidation that she inched closer to Josh. It was quickly becoming apparent that he wasn't going to be starting the conversation. He was waiting for her to say something, but she had no idea where to begin. Josh must have sensed her hesitation. He took her hand and gave it a reassuring squeeze. Digging down, she found her strength and smiled back at Collin.

"So, I was wondering how you knew my grandmother and mother," Rachel said. "I heard you were close to them both."

"Well, now, let me see. It was an awfully long time ago, you know? Though I recall meeting Patricia decades ago when I first moved to the area. There was some kind of town function for newcomers. I believe that was around the time when there were lots of folks moving to the area."

"I take it the two of you became friends rather quickly?"

"We hit it off as friends right away, but we were never romantic. It was just nice to have someone in the area to talk to since I was so new around here."

"How old was my mother when you first met Patricia and the family?"

Collin sighed. "I want to say she was fifteen, but that can't be right. I'm pretty sure she was about sixteen when I met her. I tell you what, that girl was the prettiest girl in the whole darn county. She always had all the men chasing after her."

Rachel smiled. "I've only seen a picture of her, but from what I can tell, she was a lovely woman. After you moved around here, did you stay?"

"Patricia definitely made it worth staying. So, yeah, I've been here ever since. I like the area, but a friend like your grandmother is a once-in-a-lifetime sort of thing. I never needed to be anywhere else."

"If you've been here since then, were you around when Amanda came back to stay with Patricia the last time? This would have been some time after we were born, but she died soon after."

Collin cringed and nodded, obviously upset by the memory. She felt bad for dredging it all up again, but it didn't stop her. Rachel had to get answers. Having someone to talk to about it all made her want them even more.

"I had no idea she was home, to be honest, not till the night she went and walked into the river—"

"Half of the people we talk to say she was carried away; the other half say she killed herself. It doesn't make sense," Rachel growled.

"The girl went off her rocker that night. I'll tell you that much. It isn't right to talk ill of the dead, but she came back here messed up and talking crazy that night. I'd gone to visit her momma. Hell, Patty hadn't stopped by in months, and I was worried about her."

"Why didn't she tell you my mother was back?" Rachel asked.

"Hell, I don't know. She didn't tell anyone the girl was back and sure as hell didn't mention that she had her two kids to beat. That sure came as a shock to all of us," he muttered.

"All of us?"

The man shrugged again. "The town? The people? Everyone loved little Amanda. Then she just went and abandoned all of us. Might have been some hurt feelings. Y'all should talk to that old crow, Mary West. She was always sticking her nose where it didn't belong."

She pursed her lips. They had already spoken to Mary, and she hadn't mentioned much about Collin. If nothing else, the conversation had solidified her hunch that there were secrets in the community that no one was going to let slip easily. Rachel didn't know who she was supposed to believe or trust anymore. It was an infuriating feeling. She knew she was starting to lose the man's interest in the conversation.

"What did you mean about Amanda on the night she died?" Rachel asked. "You said she was acting crazy and that her behavior wasn't normal."

"Hell, the woman was talking like a crazy person. Amanda came to me that night and sounded like she was out of her mind," Collin said.

"What did she say to you that made you think she

had lost it?"

"For starters, she was going on and on about how the estate wasn't safe anymore. If you ask me, it sounded like someone there was making her feel unsafe. I don't know, but it couldn't have been further from the truth. Y'all have been out there, right?"

"Yes, sir. We've been there for a few days now."

"Plenty of time for y'all to know there ain't nothing dangerous about the place. Maybe now anyway. The way Amanda put it made me wonder if she was scared of ole Patty, but I knew the woman too well to believe some crap like that. Might have just been the way I took it, but it sure seemed like she was scared of something; I'll tell you that."

"You're saying my mother said she was afraid of Patricia? That doesn't make any sense."

"I told you, that girl was out of her mind that night. Now, she never came right out and said it, but with everything she was talking about, Patricia was the only one she could have been talking about."

Rachel was shocked for a moment. Nothing so far had led her to believe that Patricia was the kind of woman to turn on her daughter, but she had only read her thoughts in a journal.

"Do you think that my grandmother had something to do with Amanda's death?"

Collin scoffed. "It ain't my place to say anything on the matter."

The group fell silent. She could see they weren't going to get any more answers out of the man. While he'd given them a good bit to think about, she wasn't ready to believe that her grandmother had anything to do with her mother's death. It would explain the negative entity that she felt in the house, but Patricia had adored both her husband and her daughter. Rachel simply couldn't see the kind and caring woman doing something as awful as murdering her own flesh and blood.

There was no denying that it was strange that both Patricia's husband and daughter had passed away before her. Yet she'd taken her life in the same manner as her daughter. It was a rabbit hole Rachel couldn't let herself fall down. Instead, she thanked Collin for his time and rose, indicating they were done. Josh quickly followed her back to the truck, but Collin didn't bother to stand as they slipped outside. Grabbing her phone, she texted her sister to let her know they were heading home. From the way Zach had bolted out of there earlier, Rachel could only assume the two had reconciled.

Rachel had no intention of speaking to the man again unless it couldn't be avoided. He was about as useful as she'd found Jessica to be. She wanted to get back to the estate and prepare for the medium Josh had hired for the evening. With the crypt and its answers waiting, the pair headed in the direction of Red River. She didn't know if she was ready to confront the spirits of the house, but she knew it needed to be done. None of them were going to get any rest as long as there were negative spirits waiting to sabotage them around every corner.

33

*H*ours later, as they prepared for the woman to arrive, Rachel thought about the afternoon's events. Meeting with Collin had only been the tip of the iceberg. Upon hearing about Josh and Rachel's plans to hold a seance, both Grace and Becky had abandoned the house. She didn't care that Grace didn't want to be there. From the first mention of a haunting, she'd made it clear that she wanted nothing to do with the afternoon plans. Becky, on the other hand, had acted unlike herself.

"Are you still dwelling on it?" Josh asked.

Her eyes snapped up from the drink she'd been stirring. Rachel blushed, realizing she'd been stirring the same martini for almost four minutes absent-mindedly. Josh had always been able to pick up on her moods and thoughts.

"Sorry, I can't help it. It's just so strange. Becky would normally be gung ho about doing something like this. She'd already had her phone charged and ready to film it. She spooked though…why?"

He shrugged. "I really have no idea. Maybe she's just freaked out because it's so real. This has to be a lot for her to handle. Not just the ghosts, but the money, grandmother, a mother who died and didn't abandon you…"

She sighed, knowing her partner was right. Becky had always processed things in her own way. Rachel couldn't rush her sister, and she wasn't going to force her to be there when the woman arrived. If they needed more people, she would call Mary or anyone else before reaching out to Becky. Seconds later, there was a timid knock on the front door. Her eyes darted to Josh. He quickly crossed the parlor into the foyer and answered the door. Unlike Collin Hunter, the psychic looked every bit like what Rachel had envisioned.

"Rachel, this is Madam Helena. She's the medium I talked to about coming here and talking to you about things."

"Thank you so much for coming."

"It's not a problem. From the way Josh talked about things, you needed a professional."

Rachel smiled. "Well, I don't know what's going on around here, but I feel like something is wrong."

"You're right about that," Madam Helena said. "Just from the moment or two we've been standing here, I can feel a very bad energy. It's a negative energy I can't shake, but I definitely feel it more since I've stepped into the house."

"I know. Not only have I been feeling things around here, but I've also actually seen the spirits. Can you tell me if it's my grandmother that I'm seeing?"

The woman grew quiet and paced around the immediate area. Rachel couldn't tell what she was doing, but it definitely looked as though she was making things up as she went along. It wasn't the first time she'd seen a medium act like they were doing something when, in reality, they were trying to think of something to say. Still, she was trying to stay positive about the experience in the hope that the medium would give her some kind of information about what was happening around her.

After a few more minutes of the woman walking through part of the house and touching the walls, Helena shook her head. "It's not a woman's energy that I'm feeling through the walls and in the air. It's more of a masculine one that's responding to my presence."

"My grandfather passed away here long before I was born. That's something you could have found online, though," Rachel said.

Madam Helena chuckled. "You're right, but this energy, it's reached out to you already, has it not? The chill, the dreams…perhaps waking where you don't belong?"

Rachel swallowed and nodded. She didn't doubt what the woman was picking up on, but she had to be sure Madam Helena was the real deal before opening up to her. So far, she was doing an excellent job of proving her credentials. While Rachel had already known about the angry spirit on the property, she had no idea what to do about it. The last thing she wanted was for her sister to stay in a house she wasn't safe in. The words of her mother's ghost came back to her.

"How do we get rid of it?" Rachel asked. "Jeez, I don't even like the way that sounds. I don't like any of this."

Madam Helena smiled. "You've been warned, haven't you? By the spirit, that is. It's evident something doesn't want you here, but there is more to it. Someone is trying to keep you safe as well, you and all the innocent lives that have passed through that front door. There is another here…not as strong as the dark spirit, but present nonetheless."

"My mother, Amanda Groves," she whispered.

"This spirit, it's strong. It has been working on you since you first arrive, yes?"

"Yes," Rachel croaked.

A chill ran down her spine. She was now certain Madam Helena was the real deal. From the moment she'd stepped foot on the estate, Rachel had known something was wrong. She hadn't thought about her grandfather, not even for a split second. His death there hadn't seemed like anything more than a tragic fate of Mother Nature. She didn't want to think about what it meant if he had been murdered. Was it truly possible that Patricia had done the deed herself? Or perhaps she had enlisted Mary as her accomplice. It would explain the falling out that they'd had after the man had died.

"I'm going to need to gather more things before we can do anything. You two will also need to get some things together, but we're going to need to wait for the full moon tomorrow night."

"Is there something special about full moons?" Josh asked.

Helena smiled. "Of course, dear. Everything in the system has something special about it. In this instance, the full moon will mean that the spirits will be stronger, and therefore, more active."

"Should we leave until tomorrow? I just want to make sure she's as safe as possible."

"The spirits don't actually have the power to hurt anyone, so there's no need to leave. You both will be safe while you're here. Now, that's not to say that the spirits won't try to toy with your mind and make you think you're in danger."

Rachel wanted to believe the woman, but after the incident at the river, when she lost the ability to move under her own power, she wasn't so sure. Hurting someone could come in many forms, and a spirit toying with her mind was something she wasn't all that excited about. Still, the woman was showing more and more that she knew what she was talking about. Though it didn't make her feel much better about being in the house.

"What about the things you said we need to get?" Josh asked. "How do we know what we're looking for?"

"I will email you a list of things you should pick up, but it's nothing too crazy. I promise." The woman smiled.

"Is there anything else we need to do before tomorrow?" Rachel asked.

"I would recommend not having too many people over, and if there's any way of keeping the number of people here tomorrow to a minimum, it would be for the best."

"Okay. I can't thank you enough for coming. We'll be sure to be ready for tomorrow."

Rachel was too stunned to move or walk with the pair to the door. It was strange to think that the spirits were there, watching her every move. They had to get into the crypt and find out what her grandmother had done, not only to her husband but possibly to her daughter as well. Keeping the girls out of the house, in her opinion, was paramount. No matter what Madam Helena said, she didn't want them anywhere near the angry ghost haunting the estate. Rachel hated the idea of banishing the creature. She knew it was looking for vengeance, but with Patricia already dead, what more could be done?

Justice? Perhaps, but it wasn't worth risking her sister's life over. The lives of the living would always take precedence over that of the dead. It only took Josh one look to know she needed him. He crossed the room and wrapped her in his arms. To call the afternoon harrowing was an understatement. There were calls and plans that needed to be made. On top of that, she couldn't keep Becky away from the house forever. Neither of them could be gone overnight, but she'd have Josh posted outside Becky's door all night.

"Hey, we are going to get through this," Josh promised.

She smiled up at him. "I know. I don't know what I would do without you."

"Well, you don't have to think about that. Why don't we do something fun? Let's go crack open that crypt."

Immediately, she nodded in agreement. She needed a win for the afternoon, and taking a peek inside her grandmother's world would be just that. No matter what they found, no matter who was guilty, at least they would have answers. Slipping her hand into Josh's, she led him away from the parlor and out the front door.

34

It was wonderful to be back out in the sunshine with Josh. She didn't know if it was the knowledge that they were finally going to get some answers or if it was simply being away from the house and the daunting task that came with it. Cleansing it of spirits wouldn't be easy. She had seen a few of the seances online but had never participated in them. Making their way to the cemetery, Rachel and Josh took their time as they approached. When they reached the crypt, she held on to him as she reached for her boot. He chuckled and shook his head.

"Why am I not surprised you've got it stashed in there? I take it you've got some trust issues with your houseguest?" Josh asked.

"My houseguest? I don't know about that. It still doesn't feel like my home. I feel like we are staying with Grace, honestly," Rachel muttered.

Before she could wiggle her way out of her boot,

her phone started to vibrate. Jessica's number appeared on the screen. Rachel sighed and silenced the call. It wasn't Grace or Becky, so she wasn't going to worry about it. Jessica was the last person she wanted to talk to. The woman had a way of ruining her mood every time. She needed a few minutes just to herself. Almost immediately, though, Jessica called her again. Rachel groaned and put her foot back down, the key still in its hiding place.

If the woman was going to keep calling until she answered, then it was going to be easier to get it out of the way. There wasn't a chance in hell that Rachel was going to let the woman ruin her afternoon adventure with Josh. She was anxious to crack into the crypt and find out what Patricia had been hiding. The faster she had answers, the better she would feel about Grace and Becky returning to the estate.

"Hello."

"What are you doing?" Jessica asked.

Rachel sighed. "It's really none of your business what I'm doing if we're being completely honest."

"Fine. When was the last time you saw your sister?"

Suddenly, she felt a sinking feeling in her stomach. If Jessica was asking her a question like that, then maybe something had happened to Becky. She felt like she was going to get sick, but she knew if something was going on, then her sister would let her know. Quickly thinking about when she had seen her, Rachel thought about the argument they'd had just a few hours earlier when her sister had asked if they could talk about Zach later and walked out. She figured Becky was just going to take some time to herself like she always did after they'd bicker.

"It was a few hours ago, but nothing unusual for the two of us. We can go days without talking to each other. Why are you asking?" Becky asked.

"Well, I don't know what's going on, but Grace has been blowing my phone up for the last hour."

"What is she saying?" Rachel asked. "I figured if anyone knew where Becky was, it would be her. The two have been nearly inseparable since we got here."

"That's what I'm saying," Jessica screeched. "Grace has called me several times, and all she can tell me is that Becky is missing. I figured I'd call you to see when the last time you talked to her was."

Rachel's hands were shaking. The woman was still talking on the other side as Rachel ended the call and quickly dialed her sister's number. It rang several times before going to voicemail. She tried to call it again but got the same results. Thankfully, the twins were prepared for every situation. Rachel didn't hesitate to end the call since she wasn't getting an answer and pull up the tracking application they both had on their phones. It pinged her sister's phone a few miles away from the estate.

Pulling open the satellite map of the area, Rachel's heart plunged. There was nothing in the area but forests and swamps. She was still trembling as she raced for the gates of the cemetery, Josh following her. He called out, begging her to tell him what was going on. Despite how frantic she felt, she knew he had to know what was happening. The conversation was a brief one. As soon as Josh understood the situation, he jumped into gear. While he sprinted for the house and his truck keys, Rachel called Grace to get some answers.

She wanted to believe the young woman was good at heart, but until she could be certain beyond a shadow of a doubt, Rachel was going to err on the side of caution. She had no intention of telling anyone the location where Becky's phone last pinged, not until she knew who she could trust. Why had Jessica called her and not Grace? Something was fishy, and her sister's life might be on the line. Rachel fought to keep her fear and rage under control. She had to keep a level head, no matter how she felt inside.

"Did you find Becky?" Grace asked, answering the call.

"Why didn't you get ahold of me as soon as you thought she was missing?" Rachel asked. "I'm her sister."

Grace hesitated. "I guess I just didn't want to worry you. I knew you were out doing things, but I figured she would show up by now. I haven't heard from her, and I thought maybe my mom knew something about it."

"We're out looking for her now," Josh said. "I'm not exactly sure where we're going to go next, but she couldn't have gone very far."

"Oh, thank God. I'd love to come out and help

you look for her. Do you have any idea where you're going to head off to next?"

Rachel was still angry at the girl for going behind her back instead of letting her know Becky was gone. It was hard enough for her to keep her rage under check while just being on the phone, and she certainly didn't feel comfortable with Grace going on the search with them. Not until she figured out what was going on first. Josh looked at her, and she shook her head. Instantly, he knew what to do.

"You're starting to break up, Grace. Are you losing signal, or are we?" Josh asked.

"It might be me. I don't get the best signal around here, but I usually don't have a problem with it. I was just trying to find out where you guys were heading to look for her."

"Okay," Becky said. "We'll give you a call if we find her or figure anything out."

While she knew she had ignored the girl's question twice, Rachel didn't care. She didn't want her out looking for her with the two of them. The pause on the other end made her feel a little bad about it, but the fact that Grace had gone to her mother instead of letting her know was still fresh on her mind.

"Okay, thank you," Grace whispered.

"Do you know what she was doing? Were you following her into town?" Rachel asked.

"No, I was going to check on my mom first, a little surprise, and she was going to talk with Zach. We were going to meet in town for a late lunch and then go shopping. You guys wanted some space, so we were giving it," Grace said.

"So, she was going to meet Zach? Who else knew?"

"I-I don't know, I'm sorry. I waited for her for over an hour at the diner, then when I called Zach, he said he hadn't seen her. I just panicked."

"It's fine. I'll call if we find anything."

Without another word, she hung up on Grace. By the time she reached the driveway, Josh was waiting for her with the truck running. She quickly relayed the conversation with Grace, though it was nothing more than a dead end. As they sped out of the driveway and down the road, Rachel prayed she was overreacting and her sister simply had a flat tire on the side of the road. Why had she insisted on driving everywhere in the rental car? She could have ridden to town with Grace, but the stubborn girl refused to let anyone else behind the wheel.

Minutes later, the rental car came into view, and her stomach lurched. The driver's door was standing open, with Becky's purse clearly lying on the ground next to it. Josh brought the truck skidding to a stop on the gravel as Rachel jumped out of the vehicle. The piercing sound of Becky's abandoned phone ringing from the car was the last straw. Rachel broke down, dropping to her knees as Josh ran to her. Something had happened to Becky, and she had to find out what.

35

Rachel quickly collected herself, refusing to give in to the emotional turmoil ravaging her heart and mind. If she was going to find Becky, they had to start the search right away. Josh was already looking at the satellite map on his phone, searching for any signs of a trail she might have taken. With the exception of Becky's own skidding car tracks, there were no others on the gravel road that gave her concern. Josh shook his head when Rachel gave him a hopeful look. He was coming up empty-handed. There was nothing they could do but set out on foot.

Jogging down the embankment, her eyes lowered. Immediately, she was able to make out indentations in the ground. While Rachel had almost no experience in navigating the wilderness or looking for tracks, the shape of her sister's boot was clear in the soft earth. For the first time since their arrival, she was happy for the muddy earth that surrounded the estate. It gave her hope that they might be able to find her sister before the swamp consumed the poor girl. Becky wasn't cut out for wilderness survival. What on Earth had she been doing?

"Look!" she called out to Josh. "There are footprints over here. She went this way. It looks like she was alone, too. Why in the hell would she go off into the swamp?"

"Maybe she wanted to scout the area for a video?" Josh offered.

Rachel shook her head. "She wouldn't leave her phone behind if that was the case."

Before she could head into the thick, swampy marsh, Josh grabbed her arm and held her back. Rachel spun around and glared at him. Instantly, she could see that he regretted the decision to grab her arm. If he thought for one second she was going to sit on the sidelines while he went looking for Becky, Josh had another think coming. She jerked her arm free, her eyes still locked on him. Out of everyone in the world, she'd never expected Josh to be the one keeping her back.

"Maybe we should call the police before going out on a search," Josh said.

"Becky might not have that kind of time. If she went out this way and something happened to her, we need to get to her before it gets any worse."

"That's why we should call. I mean, if she slipped and fell or got hurt in any way, we should have the authorities already on their way."

Rachel scoffed. "Are we just going to sit here and wait for the police to show up and help with the search when we could already be out there looking for her? I'm not sitting around a minute longer than we have to."

She instantly started to feel bad for the way she was jumping on him, but it was her sister they were talking about. If anything had happened to her twin, she'd never forgive herself. The weight of the world suddenly felt heavy on her shoulders. The only thing that would release some of it would be to find Becky and be sure she was all right. The police wouldn't do anything more than they could do themselves, and every minute they wasted was another minute she was out in the swamp alone.

"We don't have to waste any time other than the minute or two it will take to make the call. All we can do is look for her, but if we find her injured or caught in something we can't get her out of, I think it will be better to have someone who knows what they are doing to help find her."

Rachel sighed. "Fine, make the call. As soon as you get through, we're going to look for her."

"Thank you. That was all I was asking for. I'll put in the call, and then we can go."

Josh pulled out his phone, quickly calling the local police as they stepped into the marsh. She had read about the dangers of the Alabama swamps. There were a handful of venomous snakes, each worse than the last. Along with unchartered terrain and the possibility of getting an infection that could be fatal, Rachel knew the faster they found Becky, the better. Calling out for her sister as Josh finished giving their location to the dispatcher on the other end, she scanned the area for any further clues.

They continued to tromp deeper into the swamps, despite Josh's hesitations. After a few more minutes, the sound of sirens could be heard on the road where they'd left his car. She wasn't going to stop, though, her eyes moving across the dim landscape. Just as Josh started to protest more, insisting they turn back and regroup with the police, something up ahead caught Rachel's eye. Her heart plummeted to her stomach when she started to approach the form.

Screaming her sister's name, Rachel collapsed into the murky water next to her sister's near-lifeless body. She was barely breathing. Rachel didn't want to let her go but gave her up nonetheless when Josh swooped down and lifted Becky's limp body into his arms. He was yelling for the police, the paramedics, everyone, as Rachel raced after him. She was too shocked to do anything but pray for her sister, to pray Becky would make it through.

* * *

Rachel and Josh were waiting outside Becky's hospital room. When they rushed her into the emergency room, no one had any idea what was wrong with her. The doctor's initial workup of her sister was that she was a healthy young woman with no history of illness. Still, as the two waited to hear something from the doctor, she had no idea what to think. Her entire body was numb from seeing her sister in such a state. Suddenly, as she looked down the hallway, she noticed the doctor approaching them. Her heart jumped when she saw the look on his face, and she leaped up from the chair in haste to see what he had to say.

"Is my sister going to be okay?" Rachel asked.

"It's hard to say at this point. It's going to be a waiting game to see if she pulls through or not. For now, Becky is in a coma, and we have no idea when, or if, she'll wake up."

"What happened to her? When I spoke to her this morning, she seemed perfectly fine."

"That's the thing. I had the nurse draw her blood to do a tox screen. It's normal in cases where the patient is unconscious when they arrive to do that. I just got the results back, and it looks like she has been poisoned."

"What? What do…what are you saying?"

The doctor sighed. "Well, Becky had nightshade in her system. It's scientifically known as Atropa belladonna but commonly known as nightshade.

"How would that get in her bloodstream?" Josh asked, equally confused as she was.

"There's no way of knowing how it got into her system. It's equally as poisonous if ingested or used topically, and depending on the amount, it's hard to say when she could have been in contact with it."

Rachel couldn't believe what the doctor was

telling them. Even as he went over it all a second time, the words wouldn't register. Josh held her close, talking with the doctor as Rachel turned back to look at Becky in her hospital room. Each time she saw her sister lying there unconscious, she was overcome with grief. It was her fault Becky was there, her fault they'd stayed in Alabama at all. She no longer cared about the estate or the mystery. All she wanted was for her sister to wake up so Rachel could take her far away from it all.

The doctor shook Josh's hand before turning and walking away. Without a word, he led her back into her sister's room and closed the door as she took a seat next to the unconscious woman. The outlook was good, but they wouldn't know the extent of the damage until Becky woke up. There was no telling how long that might be. She could be out for a few more minutes or a few weeks. Either way, Rachel wasn't going to leave her sister's side. Becky was all the family she'd ever known and all the family she had left.

They were in it together, and nothing would ever change that. As a tear slipped down her cheek and Rachel squeezed Becky's limp hand, a single thought passed through her mind. Someone out there had tried to kill Becky and almost succeeded. She was going to find out who it was and make them pay. With a renewed determination, Rachel started to talk to her sister, still certain her twin could hear her. She wouldn't rest until the person responsible was brought to justice, no matter how long it took.

36

It was after five in the evening, but there had been no change in Becky's condition. Rachel was starting to doze off on Josh's shoulder when there was a knock on the door. Instantly, she was alert and standing before Grace appeared. While she was fine with the woman coming to check on Becky, the one who followed Grace into the room was not. Jessica had a smug look on her face. The third and final newcomer was not one she had anticipated at all, and his presence there explained Jessica's satisfied expression. If James, the attorney, was there, it couldn't mean anything good.

Grace was the only one of the trio who seemed to care about Becky and Rachel. She raced over to Rachel, pulling the woman into a caring embrace before asking Josh about Becky's condition. As much as she wanted to be a part of the conversation, she was still brimming with rage over the sight of Jessica and James. The legal presence was obviously only there at Jessica's bidding. Had the elderly woman been behind the attempt on Becky's life? While she wanted to jump right to conclusions, she knew Jessica hadn't been anywhere near her sister recently.

She could feel Josh's eyes on her as she grabbed hold of Jessica and escorted the pair to the far edge of the room. There was no reason for Becky to hear the choice words she had, even if she was unconscious. Rachel had spent the last few hours reading everything she could get her hands on regarding comatose patients. The belief was that they could still hear the world around them in some cases. If that were true, Rachel didn't want to upset Becky with more drama. The poor girl needed her rest. Whatever they had to say, they could tell Rachel in private.

"Are you going to tell me what in the hell you're doing here?" Rachel fumed. "My sister is lying in a hospital bed right now in a coma, and you're here as what? Caring members of the family?"

James sighed. "I know you're going through a lot right now, and I hate to be the bearer of more bad news. The problem is that the wording of the will makes it clear that you both need to be at the estate by midnight."

"What? You think I give a crap about that right now when Becky is in that room fighting for her life?"

"Whether you do or don't isn't what I'm here for. I just have to let you know if you both aren't back by that time, you forfeit your inheritance."

Rachel scoffed. "So, I see what's really going on here. Or at least I'm starting to. I don't care about the money or inheritance. We're not going to be there, and you can take that money and shove it where the sun doesn't shine."

"I do hope your sister pulls through. I mean that from the bottom of my heart."

She was fuming by the time they finished talking. It was easy to see by the look on the man's face that he was being genuine, but Rachel didn't care about that. She found herself wondering what position Jessica was trying to take on everything and whether she had something more to do with what had happened to Becky. James quickly touched Jessica's arm and guided her toward the exit. When the woman glanced back at her, she looked as though she was gloating, and Rachel was instantly filled with rage. Before they reached the door, the lawyer turned back to her with his head hung low.

"I'll be at the estate if you change your mind. You have until midnight."

As soon as the pair had left, Rachel joined the others back at Becky's bedside. She could tell right away that they had an opinion on the overheard conversation. It was her job to keep Becky safe, though, not anyone else's. Rachel took her spot next to her sister, ignoring the questioning gazes of the others. No one spoke, but she could feel their desire to intervene emanating through the silent space.

Grace cleared her throat. "You know—"

"I don't want to hear it," Rachel snarled. "There is no amount of money that will make me put my sister's life in danger again. It was a mistake to come here."

"You and I both know Becky would argue with you on that point. She loves it here. Whoever did this…it's one person who's the bad seed, not all of them," Josh said.

"So, what am I supposed to do, Josh? Just leave her here and go back for my half of the money? Maybe toss her in my car and drag her lifeless body back to the estate?" Rachel hissed the words, the rage building inside of her.

"Of course not, Rachel. I was just offering another perspective. I'm sure—"

"Please, would you both just go? Leave us in peace so I can figure out what the hell to do when she wakes up," she said.

The pair fell silent behind her, but she knew she wasn't going to get rid of them so easily. They cared about her. They only wanted what was best for both of the twins, but Rachel was determined to stay focused on her sister. As soon as they were gone, she'd take a look at the blog's finances. With what they had in savings, they could get another camper and be on the road as soon as Becky came back to her. She had to come back; Rachel couldn't fathom a world without her other half.

"Rachel," Grace said.

"What is it?"

"I know you've made your mind up on the matter, but can I at least pitch you an idea on Becky's behalf?"

Rachel sighed. "I don't care about the money. I'm starting to feel like I never should have come to Alabama in the first place."

"I understand but think about how she feels. She loves it here and has really started to take to the area."

"Okay, then, what can we do? Becky is not in any condition to be at the house, and it isn't like we can take care of her ourselves," Rachel said.

"That's what I was going to say. Patricia made a ton of donations to the hospital. She spent a lot of time ensuring they had everything they needed, including top-of-the-line equipment. Most of the staff here would be more than willing to come to the estate to take care of her there."

"Plus, if I know anything about the followers you have on your site, I'm sure they would be more than willing to donate any other supplies we might need for her care," Josh added.

"See," Grace said. "We can make this work. Now, I know you don't trust many people around here, but I'd hate to see the two of you leave here with nothing when I know it's supposed to be all yours."

"I don't know," Rachel said. "I still think she'd be better off here. Though I know she loves the estate."

"It's up to you, Rachel," Josh said. "But between

the hospital staff and your followers, we can still get Becky the best care while making sure the inheritance stays intact."

Rachel couldn't believe they were actually making sense. In a perfect world, Becky wouldn't be in the hospital room at all, but now they had to play the cards they'd been dealt. She had to admit that seeing the smug, victorious grin wiped off Jessica's face would bring her great pleasure. When Becky came back around, what was Rachel going to tell her? That she had given up everything, or that she had fought for it, just like Becky would have wanted her to?

Drawing a ragged breath, Rachel nodded to the others without saying a word. Instantly, they jumped into action. She had no idea what the pair was doing, but when Rachel was alone with her sister again, her guard slipped. How was she going to tell their followers what had happened? Even though only minutes had passed since she'd made the decision to take Becky back to the estate, she was already second-guessing herself.

There were so many things that could go wrong. Becky would need to be watched round the clock, especially with a vengeful spirit on the property, trying to end them both. Her mind was swimming. Had it been that dark force that had led Becky away or one still alive, with a beating heart? As her stomach lurched with indecision, a tear slipped down her cheek. She'd never felt so conflicted before in her life.

"What am I supposed to do here, Bec? Jesus…this is so far out of my wheelhouse," Rachel whispered to her sister. "You and I, we are a team…I can't do this without you. You have to wake up."

37

The anxiety stayed with her on the ambulance ride back to the estate. It persisted long after the hoard of doctors, aides, and nurses had Becky set up in her room. Thankfully, Josh and Grace had ridden ahead of the medical vehicle to clear out the room. Rachel was a little disappointed she wasn't there to see the enraged look on Jessica's face, but staying with Becky came first. When her sister was finally situated back in her room, the hospital bed outfitted now with the expensive estate bedding, she could finally take a deep breath again. As much as Rachel hated to admit it, she was considerably more relaxed back at the estate with Becky.

She made a mental note to thank her boyfriend and Grace for all their help. Had it not been for their persistence, Becky and Rachel would still be at the cold, impersonal medical facility. The staff had already worked out a schedule and given her a copy of it. They would make sure Becky was always tended to. Still, when there was a knock at the door, it felt wrong to be walking away from her sister to answer it. She could see the nurse and aide in the adjoining room, getting things set up for the first shift of their new job. James gave her an apologetic nod as she slipped out into the hallway to talk with him.

"I just wanted to let you know I petitioned the trust advisors on your behalf as requested," he said.

She pursed her lips. "I didn't—"

"They've agreed to release the funds needed to continue Becky's care here at the estate. You'll just need to sign off on the release of funds," James said, fishing out the paperwork.

"That won't be necessary," Josh said.

She spun around. Rachel hadn't realized he was in the hall with them as well. She'd left him and Grace in charge of everything with regard to the finances. Now it seemed he had done just that.

"What do you mean that it won't be necessary?" James asked. "It's their money to do with as they please."

"I understand that, but I think we'll have more than enough to handle all the financial needs for Becky's recovery," Josh said. "The followers on the blog have come through with everything they need. They have donated just over five-hundred-thousand dollars in the last couple of hours, and we won't need to break into anything in the trust."

"That's great news. To be honest with you."

"I never asked you to do any of that," Rachel said. "I don't understand why you would have looked into it, but I'm thankful you tried."

"It wasn't you who asked. Grace sent over an email asking for the funds. I merely did the legwork to see if we could get any of it released."

"What did she ask for?"

James sighed. "She asked for two million to be released to cover expenses, but like I said, I'm glad something else came through. Those advisors make me nervous, and you can't ever know what's going through their minds."

"Either way, thank you for telling me. I know you didn't have to do that."

"It's not a problem. The minute she let me know what you wanted to do, I knew it was the right thing. I'm glad it's going to work out that way."

"You and me both," Rachel said.

"Well, if there's anything else I can do for you, let me know. I'll stop by tomorrow to check in on Becky. I hope she recovers quickly."

Rachel could feel the rage seething through her. Her hands were balled into fists, her nails digging into the flesh of her palm. Josh quickly wrapped his arm around her shoulder, trying to ease the tension, but she couldn't seem to get it under control. It was all the confirmation she needed. Rachel had known someone was lying to her, though she hadn't been sure who was behind it. Now, knowing Grace was trying to pilfer that amount of case from the trust, she had her answer.

"Take a deep breath," Josh said.

"I'm going to rip her throat out. I thought she was busy helping us get this all setup, not trying to get money from my grandmothers' estate."

"We don't know if that's the case."

"Really? Did she mention anything about it to you? Because she sure as hell didn't say anything to me about two-million dollars," Rachel snapped.

He frowned and shook his head. "No, and I just left her in the kitchen with the rest of the hospital staff. I even told her about the money we'd raised, and she acted like she was really excited. She didn't mention talking to the trust or James at all."

"There you go, there is your answer. I'm going to kick her out of here so fast, her head will spin," Rachel said.

She stormed in the direction of the steps, ignoring Josh as he called after her. With two members of the staff in the room with Becky, Rachel felt comfortable leaving her sister alone long enough to take out the trash. Moving with determination, she didn't stop until she burst through the kitchen doors and stopped just feet from where Grace was standing.

"What do you think you're doing?" Rachel seethed.

Grace hesitated. "What are you talking about? I was just making sure the staff was aware of what we were asking them to do and keeping an eye on Becky."

"You know damn well what I'm talking about. I

want to know why you emailed James to have two million dollars released for her care."

"I would never do anything like that without asking you about it first. I never emailed James."

Rachel scoffed. "Show me your phone, then. Let me see your emails."

Grace didn't hesitate to pull out her phone and quickly pull up the emails. Immediately, Rachel could see there weren't any recent outgoing emails to the lawyer. As a matter of fact, there weren't any emails going out to James. Still, when Grace handed her phone over to Rachel, she went directly to the trash and found it. The email had been sent hours earlier, around the time they were just getting ready to leave the hospital. She quickly spun the phone around and glared at the girl.

"I didn't send that email."

"Then who did, Grace? Because it came from your account."

Grace gasped. "I know it wasn't me, but my mother has access to my email. I wonder if it could have been her."

She was instantly filled with rage, and Rachel believed her. She was already having suspicions about Jessica. Now, with the email in front of her and looking into the eyes of the woman standing in front of her, she felt like a fool.

"I'm sorry for accusing you, but everything pointed to you."

"It's okay, Rachel. I really like you and Becky, and I wouldn't do anything behind your back."

Rachel sighed. "I know, but Jessica would. Where is she now?"

"I don't know. She left about thirty minutes ago and didn't mention where she was going."

Feeling like a fool, Rachel apologized once more to Grace despite the woman living up to her name. Rachel had spoken to her in a terrible tone, yet her young friend had accepted her apology without hesitation. Jessica was behind the email, of that Rachel was now certain. She wanted to get her hands on the money, no matter what. The only question left was whether Jessica was working with someone else and just how far the woman had truly gone to stay in the estate's good graces. Thinking about her dead relatives, Rachel slowly made her way back upstairs to where her sister was peacefully unconscious in her room. Josh smiled when he saw her, noting her look of regret instantly.

"You okay?" he asked, his tone a hushed whisper.

She nodded. "It wasn't Grace. It was Jessica. I made a complete ass of myself."

Josh pulled her close. "Why am I not surprised that it was Jessica? That woman seems to be behind everything that goes wrong here. Are you and Grace okay?"

"Yeah, but I still feel like dirt. All I want is for Becky to wake up and tell me it's all going to be okay."

"Well, I don't think I can get her to wake up, but I can at least help keep you busy. You know we've still got an entire crypt's worth of secrets to unlock. Maybe it's time we finally cracked open that egg."

Rachel hesitated, her eyes moving to the pitch-black night outside. She wanted to get inside the crypt, but the thought of leaving Becky behind at the estate made her nauseous. Still, it was the only way they were going to get answers. It had to be done.

38

"Are you sure you don't mind? You've had a long day, just like the rest of us," Rachel said.

"I promise I don't mind one bit. I was going to lay in bed and read for a few hours anyway. I'll just sit with Becky and read out loud for a change. It's good for you to get out. I promise I won't leave her side," Grace said.

Rachel thanked her again before they headed for the front door. Her phone had a full charge, and she knew Grace would call if anything changed. The warm, humid air felt wonderful. Its stark contrast to the sterile scent in Becky's room was refreshing. Walking hand in hand with Josh down to the crypt gave her the terrible sensation of déjà vu. She hated knowing the last time they'd made the trek, Becky had nearly lost her life. Now, her sister was barely hanging on, and they were once again working to unravel the mystery of Red River. They didn't take any detours this time, going directly to the crypt.

Fishing the key and chain from her boot, Rachel drew a ragged breath. She slipped the key into the rusted lock, the chain swaying from it as the heavy old hinges inside gave way. They lurched with enough noise that it echoed through the trees behind the now-open door. A cold burst of stagnant air came from within, sending a chill down her spine as she glanced at Josh. He gave her a playful grin before pulling out his phone and turning on the flashlight. Rachel quickly followed suit, intrigued by what awaited them inside.

It was like nothing she'd ever seen before. The space, while only five feet deep and wide, was covered from floor to ceiling in enclosed shelving. The books that were housed there had to be worth a fortune all on their own. Rachel couldn't wait to find out what they held between the pages. Randomly placed on the shelving were a dozen knickknacks as well, though she was certain they were priceless artifacts.

Rachel opened the case and started reading down the list of author names listed on the bindings of the books. There were many of which that had been written by some of the most famous authors, and she knew they had to be worth a fortune on their own. Still, it amazed her how well they had held their integrity. Though they were out in a crypt and far from being out of the weather entirely, there wasn't a single one that didn't look in pristine condition.

Everything within the contents of the case was amazing, and she couldn't believe what she was seeing.

"Can you believe this place?" Rachel asked.

"It's truly amazing," Josh replied. "Though it looks like one of the shelves, in that case, is not quite as dusty as the others. Maybe there is something special in there."

"I'd venture to say that it's whatever Patricia was keeping."

"Whatever it is, it must have been important if she was hiding it out here. Plus, I think if she was willing to hide the key, to begin with, it's a good indication that it's something she didn't want anyone to get ahold of."

Without wasting another moment, Rachel walked to the other side of the small room and opened the case. Even though access to the case itself had been quite easy, there was a small box sitting on the shelf that was still locked. At first glance, it looked to take the same key as the crypt itself. Even after prying slightly along its edges, she knew they would need the key.

"I think we're going to need that key to open it if we want to see what's inside," Josh said.

"I left it in the door when we first came in. I'll go grab it."

She turned, her phone's flashlight still in hand, to go back to the door to retrieve the key. Rachel froze when the light landed on the door. Her stomach lurched as she frantically scanned the empty lock and surrounding ground. It was impossible. The key was missing from the lock, and worse, it was nowhere near the door on the ground.

"Everything all right?" Josh asked.

Rachel shook her head. "Did you take the key? Did you slip it into your pocket or something?"

"What? Of course not. It's yours. I don't want anything to do with it. It's almost identical to the hole in this box. I'd put my money on it being the same one."

"It was right here. I left it in the door."

"Don't stress about it; it probably just fell out. This place hasn't exactly been well-maintained. Come on, with both of us looking together, you'll have it back in your boot in no time," Josh said.

Rachel nodded in agreement as they both started to search the area for the key. She had no idea how much time had passed, but the pair didn't stop until they'd combed the grass all the way to the fence. At least an hour had passed, and still, the key did not appear. When they stood, defeated and running low on battery life, Rachel knew someone had taken the key. She had a pretty good idea of who was behind it, but she couldn't prove that Jessica was the thief. As they headed back for the house, Josh took her hand. He still had the locked box tucked beneath his free arm.

"It's all right, sweetheart. One way or another, we're going to find it. I'm sure while we were inside that a squirrel or something came along and carried it off."

Rachel sighed. "Or Jessica followed us up here and took it. I'm pretty sure she is out to get me at this point."

"I'm not saying I don't agree with you, but as far as we know, she took off several hours ago and hasn't come back."

"Maybe, but that doesn't mean she didn't sneak back somehow and follow us. I wouldn't put it past her, that's for sure," Rachel said. "She's been a pain since the day we got here."

"I hope you're wrong, for everyone's sake. Still, I'm sure it was carried off by an animal."

Rachel scoffed. "I'm not willing to take that chance. I want all the locks changed, and I certainly don't want that woman to have any access to the house or anything else on the property."

"I agree, but I don't know if we'll be able to get anyone to come out and get it taken care of right away. I promise we'll get it all switched out, but it's not going to be immediate."

"I know, but the locksmith will be willing to make an exception for this estate. I'm sure most of the town was very fond of Patricia. Just look how the staff from the hospital has helped us so far."

Josh smiled. "Well, if they won't come out and do it, I'll be more than happy to take care of all the locks myself. If it makes you feel better about being here, then we'll get it all taken care of." Josh smiled.

"Thank you. It's definitely going to make me feel better when she can't get in any longer."

There was no doubt in Rachel's mind that Josh

was a godsend. Without him at her side, she would have crumpled under the pressure long ago. It would be a cold day in hell before she let Jessica get away with stealing the key. First thing in the morning, while Josh was changing all the locks, she would be hunting down Jessica and getting back her grandmother's key. Together, they would never let anything happen to the estate or the people who called it home. She couldn't stop herself from checking on Becky, though the night aides and nurse were all keeping a close watch on her.

After giving Grace a friendly embrace, she watched her friend head into her own bedroom just down the hall. The rest of the house was quiet now. Josh had gone to each of the windows and doors to ensure they were all locked for the evening. She adored him for every small thing he did. There was no question that he was the love of her life. Watching him climb the steps, a fatigued and weary look in his eyes, she wanted nothing more than to be in his arms beneath the bedroom sheets.

Slipping into the bedroom adjacent to Becky's, Rachel fell back on the bed. Her heart ached for her sister. What sort of hell was going on inside the comatose woman? Josh pulled her into his arms when he joined her, nuzzling into her and helping to wash away all the worries and fears. Rachel knew they could make it through anything as long as they had each other.

39

She barely slept most of the night. Every hour or so, the need to check in on Becky would consume her dreams. Rachel would rise and creep down the hall the half-dozen steps to her sister's door. Each time she'd peek inside, Rachel saw the same thing. The two aides and single nurse would be tentatively tending to her sister's every need. She would climb back into bed, sure that sleep would elude her, only to find hideous dreams waiting for her on the other side. Sixty minutes later, she'd bolt back awake. Thankfully, Josh was snoring softly next to her each time.

At least one of them had gotten some sleep. When the sun moved across the floor to the bed in the morning, she was up and immediately racing down the hall to check on her sister. The only thing that had changed was the staff from the night before. The new nurse and aides greeted her warmly but gave no prognosis on Becky's condition. That would come when the doctor arrived in a few hours. She was happy to have the staff on hand, but it wasn't lost on her how much the specialized care was costing them.

A half-hour after she'd gotten up, Rachel was returning to the bedroom with two steaming cups of coffee and a small toolbox she'd found in the kitchen. If they didn't have the key, they could at least pry open the box and learn what Patricia had been hiding. It was easy to see the box had been one of her grandmother's keepsakes. It was the only place in the crypt where the dust was disturbed. Before it got too late in the day, she was going to make a trip into town and confront Jessica, no matter what Josh thought about it.

Before she could do anything with the box or talk to Josh about the plans she had, Rachel needed to wake him up. She was only returning the favor he had given her the day before when he had let her sleep in. Plus, the fact that she hadn't been able to sleep all night anyway made her the first one up. Setting the fresh cups of coffee on the nightstand next to the bed, she called his name softly to wake him for the day.

"Good morning, beautiful," Josh said. "Anything new on Becky?"

"I checked on her several times throughout the night and first thing when I got up this morning. Nothing has changed in her condition."

"Well, I feel like she's going to make some strides today. She's just as strong as you are, if not a little more stubborn. She's going to pull through this."

"I know you're right, but I hope she starts recovering soon. I can't stand the thought of her being in that state," Rachel said.

"Neither can I, but I'm keeping my hopes up about it."

Rachel sighed. "I'm trying to, but I have some things to do. I'm going to head into town."

"Okay, well, give me a few minutes to get dressed, and I'll go with you."

"No. I'd rather you stay here and keep an eye on Becky. One of us should be close by at all times."

"You're right, but I feel like you're hiding something. Are you going to talk to Jessica?"

"There are just a couple of things I need to do in town. I won't be gone for long, but I want you here for Becky. Either for if she wakes up or just to look out for her."

Josh grew quiet. "I will check in on her while you're gone."

After spending a few more minutes talking with Josh, it became clear that he was upset about her going into town alone to talk with Jessica. There was still the matter of the list they needed to procure for the medium as well. She knew he wasn't going to argue with her, no matter how much he wanted to. He would stay behind and watch Becky like she'd asked, his personal feelings aside. Climbing back off the bed, Rachel quickly got dressed and gave Josh a peck on the cheek before heading for the rental car.

She wasn't incredibly familiar with the area, but she had a general idea for where she needed to go. Jessica had told them about staying with a friend who ran a bed and breakfast. A quick internet search told Rachel there were only two possibilities in the small town. Of them, one woman seemed completely oblivious to who Jessica was. It only made sense that her grandmother's former friend would be residing at the other. Keeping the volume on her phone turned all the way up, Rachel knew her sister could wake up at any minute and didn't want to miss the call when she did.

Pulling up to the quaint house on the edge of town, Rachel quickly discovered she had presumed right when she saw Jessica's flashy car parked around the back. Climbing the steps, she stormed through the front door to a small receptionist's desk. The elderly woman looked up at her and smiled.

"Hello there. I'm looking to surprise a dear old friend of mine, Jessica Frank. She told me she was staying here," Rachel said.

The woman lit up. "Of course! She's in room number four, all the way at the top of the steps. Oh, what a wonderful surprise for her."

Rachel thanked her and quickly jogged up the steps. Drawing a deep breath, she focused her attention on the task at hand and knocked on the front door. After waiting a handful of seconds but hearing nothing on the other side, she tried the knob. Suddenly, the door jerked open, and Jessica appeared, nearly running into Rachel before she saw the woman standing there.

"What are you doing here?"

"I'm trying to find out just what you were up to last night," Rachel said. "Where did you go after you left the estate?"

"I don't think I need to explain my whereabouts to you. Actually, I really don't have to tell you anything. I had things to do, and I left. I shouldn't have to tell you anything."

"Well, even if you don't want to tell me where you were, I know you're the one who stole the key from the crypt."

Jessica laughed. "What on Earth are you talking about? I didn't steal any key, and I wasn't even at the estate after leaving. So you can take your accusations and shove them right back where they came from."

"So, you didn't take it then?"

"No, why would I? It's a crypt. Even if I wanted to get in there, I certainly wouldn't take any stupid key. Why are you so interested in that key, anyway?"

"I want to look at the family archives."

"For someone who wants to look at the archives so badly, you've certainly asked about that key enough times," Jessica said. "I don't know where it is or who has it."

"You don't feel the need to tell me where you were last night, and I'm not going to tell you anything about what I want with the key. I guess that makes us pretty even."

"I was just wondering, but I have no need to get

into the crypt. Now, if you'll excuse me, I have more important things to deal with than you."

Rachel scoffed. "I'm sure you do, but while I have you here, you should know I'm banning you from the estate from here on out."

Jessica smirked, inching closer to Rachel and towering over her in heels. "You can't keep me away from the estate. It's a big piece of property."

"You think I won't bring in security? I will have people watching your every move. You won't get anywhere near me or my family again."

She could see the venom in Jessica's eyes, but she wasn't going to back down. A flush jumped to her cheeks as Jessica backed away, slamming the door in her face. She jumped and stepped back, heading down the hall and jogging to her waiting car. They only had a few hours before Madam Helena was going to be at the property. She needed to get to the store and start making phone calls to security companies in the area. Her threat had been real. If Jessica set foot anywhere on the estate, she'd have her thrown into jail for trespassing.

Putting her car into gear, Rachel glared up at the woman's window to find her scowling down at her. The truth was right there, her instincts now on high alert. There was something in her eyes that sent a chill down her spine. The creature was a killer, no matter what evidence they did or didn't find. Her instinct told her they needed to watch their backs. Jessica was playing for keeps.

40

"I was surprised at how easy it was to find everything at that little market. They even had the sage," Rachel said.

"Huh," Josh mumbled.

Rachel sighed. "Okay, start talking. You've been acting weird since I got back. Did something happen with Grace? Did she make a move on you again?"

He shook his head but said nothing. How in the heck was she going to make things better if he refused to open up and talk to her? When she'd left a few hours before, he had seemed okay, for the most part, if not a little miffed that he was being left behind. Now, something was definitely wrong with him. Grabbing the last of the things from the bag, she snatched it off the table and stormed out of the kitchen with Josh following her.

"If you don't want to talk to me, fine, but you can go somewhere else if that's the case. I've got enough angry energy floating around this place," she snapped.

"I'm sorry, Rachel. I promise you haven't done anything wrong. This place is just getting a little crowded for me," he mumbled.

She stopped in the hall and turned to look at him. "What do you mean? Because of the staff? As soon as Becky wakes up, it will go back to just being the four of us."

He shook his head quickly. "No, no, I don't mind them at all. They are all pretty chill. It's that Zach guy lurking around Becky's room that I don't like. He said you told him he could be here?"

Her cheeks flushed. She had told Zach he could stop by and visit, but she didn't expect him to be there the entire time. Had she known, she would have made it clear the visit would need to be kept brief. Setting down the armloads of items on a side table, Rachel wrapped her arms around Josh.

"I'm sorry, Josh. I told him he could stop by to see her, but I never said anything about how long the visit could be. I didn't expect him to still be here when I got back. I'll tell Zach that he needs to leave right away."

Josh sighed. "It's not really that big a deal. It just took me by surprise, and he's been here for a while."

"Honestly, it's not just you. It makes me feel uncomfortable with him being here like that. I'm sure he cares about her, but they barely know each other."

"Yeah, just a few days, and he's hanging around like they've been together for years."

"Not for long. I'm going to let him know it's time for him to go, and if I hear anything about Becky, one of us will let him know what's going on."

Josh smiled. "While you're doing that, I'll go let Grace know Helena will be coming. At least she'll have a heads up and maybe want to be a part of it."

"I didn't think about letting her know," Rachel said. "I'm glad you did. You go and take care of that, and I'll make sure Zach knows he's overstayed his welcome. Meet me in the parlor after?"

"As soon as I'm done with Grace, I'll meet you over there."

Grabbing everything she'd put down, Rachel quickly deposited it into the parlor before taking the steps two at a time to the top. When she reached her sister's room, she found the door was already cracked open. Zach was sitting at Becky's side, holding her hand as he read the news out loud to her from his phone. He glanced up when he heard the door open. Doing her best to smile at the man as she closed the distance between them, Rachel immediately felt like something was off. It sent a chill through her body as she looked around for the danger her body had foretold, but there was nothing there.

"Hey, I was wondering if we would see you before the big show," Zach said.

"What big show?"

"The séance? Jessica told me about it. I guess she

and Grace were chatting about it the other day. So, when do we start?"

Rachel didn't reply to him right away. It was strange to her that Jessica and Grace would be talking about Madam Helena's visit, especially when Grace had made it clear she and Jessica weren't on good terms. Something wasn't adding up, but she didn t have time to pursue it. Instead, she needed to get Zach out of there so they could get ready for the woman's pending visit. The sooner she could have the house cleared of evil entities, the better it would be for all of them. Zach, the poor idiot, looked completely oblivious to the internal conflict going on inside of her. Glancing past him to her sister, she was almost certain for a split second that she saw Becky's eyelids flutter.

"Look, Zach, I appreciate you caring enough to come to check in on Becky, but the séance is a private meeting with Madam Helena. It's time for you to leave. I promise if Becky's condition changes in any way, one of us will let you know."

"Oh, I'm sorry," Zach said. "Jessica brought it up, and I've always been fascinated with that sort of thing. Anyway, let me know if anything happens with your sister."

"I promise I will," Rachel replied.

"If I don't hear anything from you, when can I come back again?"

"There's no chance that I won't call you. Even if her condition doesn't change, I'll be sure to get ahold of you and let you know when you can visit. For now, we need some time alone."

"Okay, that will work. Thank you."

Rachel nodded and waited for him to leave. After a few moments, he hadn't made a move for the door, and the longer she watched him, he seemed not to want to leave. She was already aggravated with him being there as long as he had been, but she was trying to be polite as possible. After all, her sister had a connection with Zach. She didn't want to do anything that would jeopardize that for Becky. After another minute of waiting, it was obvious he wasn't going to leave without being told again.

Rachel sighed. "It's time for you to go, Zach. I need some time alone with my sister, and Helena will be here shortly."

"Oh, sorry. Of course, I'll leave. I guess I just needed you to be more direct. All I can think about is Becky and hoping she recovers. I think I was just lost in thought. I'll be going now, but you promise you'll let me know how she's doing?"

"I swear. No matter how she is doing later, I will let you know. Now go, please."

"Thank you, Rachel. If she wakes up before I get the chance to come back, let her know I was here and thinking about her."

"I will. Now go. I'd like to visit my sister."

She watched him head for the door, not turning back to Becky until the door was closed behind Zach, with him on the other side. Immediately, Rachel turned her attention back to her sister, going to her bedside and taking the woman's hand in hers. Once again, her twin's eyes fluttered but remained closed. It brought hope to Rachel that sent her heart racing.

"Becky?" Rachel whispered. "Becky, are you in there?" She sighed, her head dropping. "I don't know what the hell I'm thinking. We never should have come to this place. I just…I need you to wake up so we can get the hell away from here."

The minutes passed slowly by, but Rachel didn't care. She waited and watched her sister, praying for any sign that Becky was going to wake soon. It wasn't until she heard the chime of the front doorbell that she managed to pull herself away from her sister. The doorbell chimed again, irritating her a bit that Josh hadn't answered it yet. Jogging out into the hall, she called for her boyfriend but got no response. She reached for the door and pulled out her phone at the same time. If he was somewhere in the back of the house, he wouldn't hear her.

Inviting the woman into the house, Rachel showed her to the parlor and quickly excused herself. She could hear Josh's phone ringing from somewhere in the back, but he still wasn't answering it. Nearly forty minutes had passed since they'd parted ways. Pushing open the swinging door of the kitchen, her heart pounded in her chest. Josh's phone was sitting on the counter, but he was nowhere in sight Rachel's stomach lurched. It wasn't like him to leave it behind. Something fishy was going on.

41

"We need to find him," she hissed. "He wouldn't leave his phone behind."

Madam Helena pursed her lips, rolling Josh's phone over and over in her hand before shaking her head. She had been on edge ever since her arrival but refused to tell Rachel why. It was infuriating to her, but she'd known her fair share of empaths and mediums in her day. They could always pick up on the unseen in an eerie way that couldn't be defined. Still, they needed to call the police and alert them to Josh's abduction. He would never abandon her minutes before they cleansed the house.

"He is safe—of this, I am sure," Madam Helena said. "You must believe me on this, child. The immediate danger is the house itself, which Josh is not a part of now."

"Wh-what the hell does that mean?" she stammered.

"It means that for better or worse, Josh is not at the estate right now while a very dark and evil spirit is, along with your ailing sister, if I'm not mistaken?"

Rachel hated that the woman was right. They needed to get whatever was lurking in the house out of their home and their minds. It wasn't going to do her sister any good if she raced off to find Josh. As soon as they were free from the evil entity, she would call the police and find her partner. Not wanting to waste any more time than they already had, Rachel followed Madam Helena back to the parlor. The room had been transformed with the two-dozen candles Rachel had been tasked with buying.

Walking into the room, each one flickered to life despite the medium not touching a single flame. A chill shot down her spine as she sat down across from the woman. Immediately, Madam Helena reached out and took Rachel's hands in hers. A single candle burning with an assortment of herbs around it sat between the pair. Its flame was low, glowing with a neon hue Rachel had never seen before. There was something unnatural about its light, a link to the woman across from her that she couldn't explain.

"I can feel something here," Madam Helena said.

"What do you mean, you can feel it?"

"I mean that we are not alone at this moment. I can sense something very close to us, and I believe the spirit is here with us now."

Rachel could sense something as well, but

without the training that Madam had, she couldn't place it. Still, as the woman continued to call out to the spirit, her heart was racing. Had she known what to expect, the pounding and ringing in her ears wouldn't have come as a shock. Helena called to the spirit again.

"Spirit, if you are here and can hear me now, it's time for you to go and be free. There is no more need for you to stay in this realm."

For a moment, there was nothing, until Rachel felt the entire room grow chilled. It suddenly felt as though they had been thrust into the arctic, and she felt the coldness in her bones. Immediately, she began to shiver uncontrollably. She couldn't believe what was happening, but Madam Helena kept pushing the spirit further.

"You're not wanted here. Whatever or whoever you are, it's time for you to be gone from this house forever," she commanded.

Suddenly, they were plunged into darkness, every candle snuffed out by an unseen force. There was only the scent of scorched wicks reminding her of the room they were in. Madam Helena squeezed her hands with such force she almost screamed out. Rachel knew the spirit was there. They were not alone in the black. She wanted to let go of the woman's damp palms, but she was frozen in place, unable to move or even breathe as the darkness closed in on her. Madam Helena was still chanting, her words fighting against the force as Rachel's stomach churned. She could feel the hatred the spirit held for her, for all the women in the house. The flame between them flickered, a faint glow bringing light and hope back to the room.

"I've never had this happen before, but there's nothing I can do to make the spirit go away," Helena said. "It's just too powerful for me."

"What am I supposed to do now?" Rachel asked. "There has to be a way."

"It's never going to happen. I don't know how or why, but this entity is stronger than any I have ever come across. I think the best thing for you to do at this point is to get out of the house and never come back here again."

"I can't do that. No matter what is going on around here, I can't just leave."

"If you don't, then you will die."

Rachel paused. "Is there nothing we can do to stop it? I mean, there's always a way when it comes to the afterlife, right?"

"The power this spirit has in this world is immense. Like nothing I have ever heard of. There's nothing you can do but run, and if you're not going to do that, then you're going to die along with everyone else here at the estate. If you don't go now, all you know will be gone forever."

Madam Helena's eyes shifted to Rachel. What she saw there made her gasp. She tried to recoil away from the pitch-black gaze now staring back at her, but the woman wouldn't let go of her. It was no longer the medium embodied within the woman across from her. Instead, it was the darkness. The entity haunting them had taken hold of the empath's form. The dark force started to laugh, Madam Helena's body trembling as she fought to regain control and cast out the evil creature. Rachel couldn't speak, her jaw slack as a thin line of blood trickled out of Madam Helena's nose. She had to break the spirit's hold on the woman before it was too late.

"You're killing her," Rachel screamed. "Let her go, please. For the love of God, just release your hold on her."

The spirit laughed. "God has no bearing on this world. I hold the power here, and I do as I please. It's too late for this witch now that I have control over her."

The voice was Helena's, but there was now a growl and deepness to it that wasn't there before. It instantly made Rachel quiver with fear. She had never been in a situation like that before, and something told her that she needed to move. When she tried to do anything, fear held her in place.

"Please, just stop this. No one here has done anything to you. There's no reason to hurt her or anyone else," Rachel stammered.

"It no longer matters who has wronged me. As I already said, it's too late for her. It's too late for all of you now. I'm going to finish you all, and there will not be any escape. Each one of you is going to die here, and I'll bask in the blood of all who dare to try to stop me."

Her eyes darted to the doors, but the ghost was

ready. By some unseen force, the large double doors slammed shut, the vibrations echoing throughout the room. She finally managed to jerk her hands free as the creature cackled, a steady stream of blood now dripping from the woman's nose onto the table in front of them. Rachel knew something else had joined them as the pain in her chest started to ease. A handful of the candles flickered back to life as she started to regain her composure. Madam Helena slumped forward, groaning softly as the darkness faded from her eyes.

"There…there is another here, someone trying to protect you," Madam Helena whispered.

"My mother—"

Madam Helena screamed, the chilling sound shocking Rachel as she leaped to her feet and stumbled for the door. She wanted to reach out and help the woman, but the dark spirit now had her in its grasp entirely. The empath was lifted from where she'd been sitting, the blood now pooling beneath her as it seeped from her nose, her lips, and her ears. The dark spirit continued its torture of the medium until the screaming and horrifying sight was too much and Rachel crumpled to the floor, covering her ears as she squeezed her eyes shut.

As quickly as the screaming had started, it stopped again. For several seconds, Rachel refused to move or open her eyes even after the room was plunged into silence. It was only when she heard Madam Helena's soft groans that she finally managed to muster the strength to get up and open her eyes. When she did, Rachel gasped. The room was in shambles, and the medium was lying on the floor, quickly approaching death.

42

Her mind was still swimming. For the first time since arriving at the estate, she was incredibly grateful for the friendships she'd made while there. While the police swarmed the house and the ambulance raced off with Madam Helena, Rachel was struggling to keep her composure. Zach was upstairs with Becky and the staff, while Grace stayed glued to Rachel's side while she spoke to the police. In the forty minutes that they'd been there, she'd managed to avoid giving her statement. They were still searching for Josh, though they refused to file a formal missing person's report for the man.

According to the detective, who seemed to be running things, Josh was little more than a traveling drifter with no home address. His absence was the least of their concerns. She still had her hands wrapped around herself as she watched the vehicle carrying Madam Helena away. The paramedics hadn't looked optimistic about the woman's outcome. Now, as the flush-faced detective stormed in their direction, she started to tremble. What in the hell was she going to tell the guy? He would never believe her if she told him the truth.

Even playing through the events in her mind made Rachel feel slightly insane. The spirit had taken hold of the woman, completely ripping her apart from the inside. She drew a ragged breath as Grace wrapped a comforting arm around her. Knowing her friend was there gave her strength. For a split second, she felt a spark of optimism. It was short-lived. A set of familiar headlights appeared in the driveway. Her stomach plunged, her heart filling with rage as Jessica's car came to a stop a few feet from where they were standing.

Instantly, Grace jumped into action, racing to intervene before there was more bloodshed. Rachel was ready to rip Jessica to shreds, but the detective was closing in on her. She knew she had to talk with him before the man would leave her alone.

"I'm going to have to ask you a few questions," Detective Whitten said. "The most obvious question I have for you is, what in the hell happened here?"

"Even if I was completely honest with you about everything that just went on, you wouldn't believe me," Rachel muttered. "No one would believe it."

"Listen, young lady, this is definitely not my first time being called out to this house, so why don't you just give me a try. I might surprise you."

Rachel sighed. "Fine, but I'm telling you, it's

crazy. Madam Helena was helping me rid the house of spirits. I'm almost positive the spirit she was trying to banish was that of my grandfather. Unfortunately, the spirit was too strong for her."

"Back when old man Groves was around, my father was the sheriff here. From what I can remember when my father would tell me stories, he was a mean and nasty man who did some of the most outrageous things. My old man used to tell me that your grandfather kept a switch in a little wooden box, and he would use it on Patricia when he felt she had gotten out of line."

"I hadn't heard any of that before, but then again, not much has been said about the man."

"My father told me a lot of stories about him, but I don't think this is the right time to tell you all of them."

"I'm not sure I want to hear all of them, either."

Detective Whitten smiled. "I understand. Listen, there's not much I can do for you about the spirit or ghost, but I'll make sure to keep an officer on hand for you through the night. Just in case something else happens."

"Thank you," Rachel replied.

She couldn't believe what the detective had told her. The small box that they'd found in the crypt, the one now hidden beneath her mattress, had to be the same as the one in the detective's story. Of course, there was no way of confirming her suspicion, not as long as the key was missing and Josh along with it.

Her heart lurched, wondering if he was okay. She knew in her gut that Josh hadn't simply disappeared from their lives. He would never leave her there alone with everything going on. Josh's phone was still sitting in the kitchen.

One by one, the officers left the property until the only person left that she wanted gone was Jessica. Even Zach, with his overbearing nature, was fine being at the estate, but she wasn't going to allow Jessica there. Grace had done a wonderful job of keeping her mother at bay while Rachel had spoken with Detective Whitten, but now that the police were gone, Rachel knew a confrontation was coming. She was ready for it. If the woman was going to drive out there for no other reason than to snoop, Rachel was done playing nice.

Even if it meant dragging Jessica to the end of the driveway by the braid of her hair, Rachel would do it. She wouldn't spend another night at the estate as long as Jessica was there. Balling her hands into fists, Rachel silently promised herself that she wouldn't stop until Jessica understood that she wasn't welcome there, nor would she ever be. Rachel was convinced she knew more about Patricia's and Amanda's death than she was letting on.

"You need to leave, and you need to do it now," Rachel fumed.

Jessica smiled. "I'm not going anywhere. I have just as much right to be here as you do. I was just coming over to make sure everyone was all right, but now I think I'm going to stick around just because you're not in charge of what I do."

"You're right. I'm not in charge of you and what you do, but I am in charge of the estate, and you're no longer welcome here."

"I guess we'll just have to see about that, won't we?"

"I don't know what your problem is, but I've had enough. You should know I have the box that Patricia was hiding in the crypt. I know for a fact that she was hiding in there for a reason. I'm going to figure out what you're hiding, too. I'm going to learn about it all."

Jessica scoffed. "I don't know what you think you're going to learn, but it's not going to matter by the—"

"It does matter," Rachel seethed. "You're not welcome here, and I think you should go before I have the police escort you off the property. Oh, and by the way, we've had all the locks changed."

She turned around and headed toward the front door. Rachel was done arguing with the woman, and she knew it wouldn't be long before she would have the answers she was looking for. It wasn't until she reached the door that she realized that Grace was a step behind her. Opening the door, she let the girl walk through first before turning around one last time to address Jessica.

"I believe we're done here. I don't want to see you back on the estate again," Rachel said as she entered the house.

Closing the door behind her, she locked the top and bottom. Thankfully, Josh had replaced them before going missing. She had no intention of giving up on finding him. As soon as it was light enough outside, she'd be combing the swamps and forests for him, enlisting every last follower they had in the area until he was found. There was nothing she could do in the darkness. Grace was quietly standing at her side still. She was a true friend, no matter what Zach had said. Rachel wrapped her arm around Grace and sighed.

"Are you okay?" Rachel asked her.

"Me? Come on, are you really worried about me right now? Your sister's in a coma, your boyfriend's AWOL, and your dead, angry grandfather just tried to kill a woman."

Rachel chuckled. "Yeah, but Jessica isn't my mother, so…"

"Fair," Grace said. "I guess I am the one who picked the haunted house and chaos over crashing with my mother so that says something about how I feel."

"Let's not worry about it tonight. Why don't you go tell Zach it's time for him to go? You and I can do a movie night on the sofa in Becky's room, a sleepover," Rachel said.

Grace's eyes lit up. She didn't want anyone sleeping alone at the estate until they knew how to exterminate the evil spirit. The pair headed up to the second floor, leaving the wrecked parlor for the morning. As she watched Grace slip into Becky's room, Rachel quietly ducked into her own bedroom. Grabbing her pillows and the blanket, she fished out the box from beneath the mattress and shoved it into her pillowcase. By the time she emerged again, Grace was closing the front door after Zach and jogging back up the steps to join her.

43

No matter how she tried to keep the mood light as the pair set up a makeshift bedroom on the sofas for the evening, Rachel's mind was racing. Her sister hadn't stirred again, taking all hope she had of a quick recovery and flushing it down the drain. As soon as they were settled in and a movie was playing in the background, the weight of the day started to sink in. Hopefully, someone would give her an update on Madam Helena's condition. Plus, Josh was out there somewhere, likely hurt or drugged, possibly worse. Rachel wasn't sure how much more she could take.

Clutching the box in her hands, she let out a weighted sigh. It was obvious that Grace was interested in the box, but her friend was too polite to ask about it. She adored the young woman for sticking by hers and Becky's side. Together, they would figure out what the hell was going on. It was going to be a tough conversation. Grace's mother had something to do with the pain and suffering the Groves family had endured. When the spirit had entered Madam Helena, its force had lost hold over the auras in the house. Her instinct told her that Grace was on their side just as sure as Jessica was acting against them.

One woman couldn't be capable of all the bloodshed at the estate. Had she worked with Patricia's husband in the deed? Is that why his spirit still lingered? Had she murdered him in a lover's rage? She shook her head and turned the box over again in her hands. Its contents rolled around inside, taunting her with each tumble. Grace was engrossed in the movie, but Rachel needed answers, even if that meant bringing in her friend on the mystery.

"I can't hold back any longer on the mystery of this box, and I can see you've grown some interest in it as well," Rachel said.

"Well, I can't deny that I was wondering about it, but I know it's really none of my business."

"I'm going to make it your business right now." Rachel smiled. "I just can't stop thinking about it. So, I'll tell you that I found it in the crypt. Patricia left it there for one reason or another. It's something she was keeping a secret, but I think it has something to do with the killer."

"You really think that the answer to who did these things is in there?" Grace asked.

"It makes sense after everything that happened tonight. I mean, I can't help but think that whatever is in this box is also the reason my grandfather's ghost is still here."

"If you think the key to figuring all of this out is in that box, then why haven't you guys opened it yet?"

Rachel sighed. "Unfortunately, while Josh and I were in the crypt, someone stole the key out of the lock on the door. I don't have any other way of getting it open."

Grace smiled. "I have the ability to unlock just about any lock that's out there. If you want, I can pick it for you."

"How in the world did you learn something like that?"

"When you're stuck going to boarding school for most of your life, you learn a thing or two about getting out. I used to pick the locks there all the time, just so I didn't have to be trapped in the building twenty-four hours a day."

Rachel laughed and handed the box to her friend. If that was something she had known sooner, they would have already had the conversation. Still, it brought her comfort, knowing they might be able to find out its contents. It was something she had been wondering about from the moment they had found it.

Leaving Grace to focus on the cryptic box, Rachel made her way across the room to where her sister was lying in the hospital bed. Each time she saw Becky, her heart lurched with guilt. How much longer would her sister be able to hang on? She needed to find a way to get through to the woman, no matter what it took. Thinking about the spirit that had assaulted Madam Helena, she had to wonder what else it was capable of doing. No, her sister had been in the coma long before they'd returned to the estate.

"Do you have a bobby pin?" Grace asked from the sofa.

She nodded, tugging one out of her bun and jogging back over to give it to Becky. "You got lucky; I don't normally have one with me."

"So, why do you have one now?"

Rachel chuckled. "When the RV caught fire, some of my hair got singed in the process. I have to keep that part pinned back; otherwise, it's constantly in my face."

"You know, this might actually work," Grace said.

Rachel returned to her sister's side once again. She wasn't going to get her hopes up anymore. Each time she did, she felt like she got slapped right back down by karma. Though it was possible that the creature was now keeping Becky trapped there. She felt like she was going to be sick. If Becky's condition had been worsened by being at the estate, Rachel would never forgive herself. Taking the seat next to her sister's bed, Rachel took Becky's hand in hers and dropped her head. It felt like an eternity since she'd last heard Becky's playful voice. The last time they'd spoken, it had been bickering over Zach. The man certainly had a way of always being in the picture.

While she was holding her sister's hand and bowing her head, Rachel felt connected to Becky in a way that she could work things out in her head. She tried to convey the conversation she was having to herself in her mind with the woman whose hand she held.

She knew Jessica would have to have an accomplice. There wasn't any chance she could have accomplished the evil she had done on her own. Although James was older than she was herself, he was still too young to have been a part of the woman's earlier sins. No matter how hard she tried to think about the people she'd met, none of them seemed to be close to the woman. Knowing how Jessica's attitude could be firsthand, it was going to be hard to find anyone who'd deal with her.

Collin's name flashed through her mind, and she began to wonder how well they had known each other. He was old enough to have helped Jessica with things all those years ago. Rachel knew she was going to need to do a lot more digging into things. Starting with the man she had only met once. Somehow, she knew Collin was going to be the key. Out of everyone she had seen come to go from the estate or surrounding area, he was the perfect partner in crime. Or, at the very least, would have some kind of answer.

Rachel laughed quietly. "What do you think,

Becky? Am I on the right path or just losing my mind?"

Rachel chuckled and shook her head, knowing her sister would give no reply. How could she when she was unconscious, only her body still fighting to keep her alive? She fell silent once again, wondering how long she could keep up the ruse of not being worried about if her sister would ever wake up.

"I'm starting to wonder if this place isn't cursed," Rachel muttered.

"Are you kidding me?" Grace asked from the sofa. "I know it is. How else could all this terrible stuff really be happening?"

"Trust me, you don't want to know my theory about all that. I'm just so worried about Josh, about Becky—if she never wakes up—I don't know what I'll do," Rachel whispered.

"Hey now, don't be thinking like that. I've only known you two for a little while, but Becky is one hell of a strong woman. She's a fighter. Whatever happened to her, I have to believe that it's not going to be the last we hear from her."

"Thanks," Rachel said.

The pair fell silent as Grace turned her attention back to working on the box. If her friend could get it open, they might be able to free themselves of the dark spirit. The house would mean nothing to her, with or without the spirits there, if she lost her sister. Closing her eyes as a tear slipped down her cheek, she squeezed her sister's hand and silently prayed once again. Suddenly, she felt something in her palm, a slight movement of her sister's fingers. Her eyes darted open, moving to her sister's face as she gently squeezed Becky's hand again.

"Becky?" she whispered.

Her sister's eyes fluttered open, searching around until they landed on Rachel.

Rachel gasped.

44

"Where am I?" Becky stammered. "I… what happened?"

"Take it easy," Rachel said.

"Holy cow, do you want me to get the nurse back here? Call the doctor?" Grace asked.

Rachel shook her head. "No, none of that yet. Let's just take a minute. How are you feeling?"

"Shit. I feel like shit. Like I got hit by a bus, dragged through a thornbush, and tossed around. Why am I in this awful bed?"

"It's a long story. I know there is a lot to take in, but we need to know what happened to you. Why were you on the side of the road?" Rachel asked.

Becky shook her head. She'd already fished the long tube out of her nose, much to Rachel's horror. She shouldn't have been surprised. Becky couldn't stand having things protruding from her. It was sheer luck alone that she hadn't noticed the IV in her other arm yet. While she knew they needed to get a doctor to the estate to look over Becky, she just wanted a few minutes to talk with her sister and rejoice in the fact that she was awake again. It would be a long time before she let her twin go to sleep without worrying.

"I was so mad at you for stepping in like that with Zach…and Grace, man…I believed everything he said."

Her heart plunged. Finally, they were going to get some answers. Grace had moved to the seat across from Rachel. She was still working on the antique box's lock but was listening with rapt interest as Becky spoke. Rachel gave her sister time to process everything, her gaze moving to Grace as the tears rolled down Becky's cheeks. She could tell that whatever had happened in the swamps had scared her sister.

"Just start from the beginning and take your time. It's okay now," Rachel said.

"Well, I was just driving down the road, not going anywhere in particular. I just wanted to get out and think about things. I wasn't that far away from the estate when I saw Zach's car on the side of the road." Becky paused.

"What happened when you stopped?"

"I thought he might have been having issues with the car, and I already felt bad about missing breakfast with him. So, I stopped to see how I could help or if he needed a ride. That's when he told me it wasn't starting. I stayed with him for a short while, but he still wasn't having any luck.

"Did he say anything that made you wonder what was happening?" Grace asked.

"No. Everything seemed to be normal. We were even joking around and talking about things we could do later. He got into the car and we were talking for a little while longer when I took a few drinks from his flask, then everything went blank."

Rachel was having murderous thoughts at that point. While she wasn't sure about much, she knew the man hadn't been entirely honest with her sister about his intentions. While Becky took a deep breath and tried to collect her thoughts, she reached over and took her hand.

"Do you know what happened after that?"

"Sort of," Becky replied. "I don't know how long it was before I woke up again, but I was in the swamp when I did. Everything was blurry, and for a moment, I didn't even know where I was. Zach was there, and he said he had something that would help with the headache I had. When I ate it, though, everything went black again soon after. Next thing I know I'm waking up here."

Rachel sighed. "He offered you a poisonous plant. That's what you ate."

"I can't believe he tried to kill me," Becky whispered. "I'm going to murder that son of a bitch."

"Easy now. I want to take him down as much as you do, but we need to be careful about this," Rachel said.

Suddenly, there was a loud pop, and both of the twins jumped, turning their attention to Grace. The sound had been the lid finally giving way. Grace's eyes grew large. Immediately, she handed the box over to Rachel. Taking it carefully in her hands, she set it on the bed between the three of them. She quickly explained to her sister what the box was and where they had found it, along with her suspicions about Jessica. Now that she knew Zach was involved in things, it was one more piece to the puzzle.

Carefully lifting the lid, Rachel gazed into the box. There was a small leather notebook tied with a thin strap. Long strips of leather with crusted blood throughout caught her attention. Lifting out the journal, she trembled at the sight of the whip. It was far crueler than anything Rachel could have imagined. Along with the small journal and whip, there was a lock of hair with a pink ribbon tied around it. A petite tag identified it as her mother's hair, taken from her first trimming at the age of five. Patricia must have treasured it to have kept it over the years.

Moving back to the journal, she opened it and quickly read through the writing. As she did, her hand flew to her mouth. It was a detailed account of her grandmother's final months on Earth. She was shocked at the amount of time and money that the woman had invested in discovering the truth. The others were waiting and watching her as she cleared her throat, wondering how to start the conversation.

"What is it?" Grace asked.

"Patricia never believed her husband died from a heart attack. She struggled with the choice for a while before finally deciding to have his body secretly exhumed."

"Oh, my God," Becky said. "You have to really believe something bad had happened to make a choice like that. Does she talk about the results of that?"

"Yes, she does. Everything looked as though the man had a heart attack until they started to look a little deeper and found out that he had nightshade poisoning. Someone had poisoned the man she loved. After that, she started to piece more together about the things around her. She was worried when Amanda never came back but never believed her daughter had committed suicide."

"That had to be so hard on her, with no one around to trust. No wonder she hid everything. Patricia didn't know if there was anyone she could tell."

"It couldn't have been easy, but according to this, she definitely didn't trust Zach. She never says anything about why, but she felt as though he was just shady about things. After some time of watching him, Patricia began to notice that he was hanging around Jessica more often."

"That makes anyone untrustworthy," Grace said.

"You know, that's still your mother," Becky said.

"Yeah, and I know now what she might be capable of."

Rachel smiled. "Fair enough. It might come as a shock to you, but our grandmother was starting to suspect the two of them were having an affair.

Though she never was able to gain any proof of that."

The conversation died down as she continued to scan the journal. Her grandmother had gone as far as researching how to eliminate the angry spirit of the man who resided in the house.

"It's all here...it looks like I was on the right track. We have to burn the whip. Patricia thought that it was the item keeping him connected to the world of the living. She believed it was the only way to get rid of him."

"Jeez, it sounds like our grandmother was a badass," Becky muttered. "All right then, does anyone have a lighter? Match?"

Rachel chuckled. "I don't think we need to do it in here. Let's wait until the morning when we can do it outside. Plus, you're the pot smoker here. Don't you have a match or two?"

Becky giggled and nodded, indicating there was a pack in the nightstand to her right. Suddenly, the lights started to flicker, the room's temperature dropping a few degrees as Rachel shivered. She carefully set down the journal and reached into the box for the whip. As soon as her fingers touched the cold metal and hide, she felt nauseous. There was definitely something dark linked to the object.

"Does anyone else feel sick?" Grace asked.

Both twins nodded. Something else was in the room with them, and all three of them knew it. She wanted to grab them both and flee from the house, but Becky was in no shape to run, given her condition. Maybe waiting to banish the spirit until the morning wasn't such a good idea after all. Without warning, a chill took over the room as they were plunged into darkness. The dark entity was back, and it came with a vengeance.

45

Knowing what was waiting for them after witnessing firsthand what the spirit could do, Rachel sprang into action. Outside, a storm moved closer to the house, flashes of lightning illuminating the room every few seconds. Fumbling around in the dark, Rachel managed to find the box of matches that her sister kept stashed there. With the next flash of light, a figure appeared at the end of the room, standing in front of the window and glaring at the trio. A chill moved through her body, the smell of rotting flesh stinging her nostrils.

She didn't hesitate, grabbing the whip from the box and tossing it on the floor as she pulled out a match. She struck it once, twice, against the box before it flickered to life. As the evil spirit screamed out and lunged for her, she let the match slip from her fingers, tumbling to the whip and igniting it with enough fury that the flames jumped two feet high. Immediately, the decaying ghost of her grandfather stopped in its tracks, screaming in agony and rage as the flames consumed it at the same speed as they consumed the whip. As the creature's only tie to the living world burned, so did its powers.

As quickly as the spirit had appeared, it was gone again. This time, though, Rachel knew it would never return. Thanks to Patricia, the twins would never need to worry about the ghost of their grandfather hurting anyone they cared about. She knew they weren't out of the woods yet. The lights flickered back to life, and she was relieved to see her sister and Grace unharmed, if not a little shaken. Instantly, she felt the presence of something else, someone in the room. Spinning around, Rachel glared at the pair standing in the doorway. It was all starting to come together. Zach leaned against the door, but it was the shotgun in Jessica's hand that had her attention.

"Why did you kill Patricia's husband?" Rachel asked.

Jessica smiled. "Well, aren't you a whole lot smarter than I gave you credit for? Since you're not going to make it out of her alive, I guess I can tell you. See, we had an affair. Honestly, I thought I loved the man, but he had other plans. He wanted to tell Patricia what we had done, and I couldn't have that getting around town."

"So, you did it to keep your reputation intact?"

"Something like that."

"What about our mother? What did she ever do to you?"

"The thing about money is that when you finally get your hands on it, you only want it more. Amanda knew I was trying to stay close to Patricia for the inheritance. Not only that, but the crumbs she handed out to us were all I had at the time. When Amanda came back, I knew I needed to handle it."

"How could you do that, Mom?" Grace asked. "After everything you tried to show me growing up, I find out you're nothing more than a cold-blooded killer."

Jessica laughed. "Do you really think the life you've had was cheap? I wanted you to have everything I never had, but you were just as greedy as I was. So, don't you dare try to act innocent."

"You really are fucking crazy, aren't you?" Becky seethed.

"I'm not the only guilty one in this room. You see, Zach here took care of dear old Grandma for me, so I didn't catch any more heat. He's a good man for a murderer."

Zach smiled. "Of course. Anything for you."

Grace scoffed. "You don't get to sit there and act like you did any of this for me. Especially when you started this rampage long before I came along."

"I swear this was all for you. Yeah, I might have wanted some of it for myself before I died, but I was planning on leaving it all to you. You can have everything you ever wanted and never have to beg on the streets," Jessica said.

"I've already found what I want from life, and it has nothing to do with you. I hope you rot in hell for the things you've done. You and that coward who calls himself a man standing next to you."

The woman cocked her gun, leveling it at Grace's chest. Rachel couldn't believe what she was seeing. The woman was truly evil. Before she could pull the trigger, though, Jessica froze. A chill moved through the room as two spirits appeared behind the murderers. Rachel didn't turn when she heard her friend and sister gasp, Becky, whispering their mother's name in the process. For a split second, a matching look of confusion crossed Jessica and Zach's faces, but the woman must have sensed they were no longer the center of attention. She turned slowly, the weapon dropping to her side as she and Zach started to back away from the entities slowly.

There was nowhere for them to go, though. The killers were trapped. In one fluid movement, both spirits lunged forward, grabbing hold of the living monsters with enough force that Rachel could hear bones breaking. The blood-curdling screams the pair emitted were horrifying. She covered her ears, unable to watch as they were dragged from the room. Rachel didn't know what to do. She could see the others were completely horrified and shocked right along with her. No matter what they had done, no matter the blood on the pair's hands, she couldn't let the spirits take them without at least trying to save them. They deserved justice, not death.

"Can you walk?" Rachel asked her sister.

Becky nodded, though the color had drained from her face the same as Grace's. She knew they were completely dumbfounded by what they had just witnessed. Not only had Grace seen her mother's dark, murderous side, but Becky had also seen their mother as a spirit. It was no longer a shock to Rachel, but she remembered the sensation and fear well. Becky pulled the IV from her arm, setting off all the alarms, but no one cared.

With her arms around Grace and Rachel, they managed to get Becky to her feet. While she was weak, she was capable of moving on her own after the others as they went down the steps and out the open front doors. It wasn't hard to tell where the spirits were going or to follow their trail. The path of blood moved beyond the porch and out into the yard. Though the storm had passed, it left behind a harrowing humidity. The sounds of screaming pleas carried across the swamp. As they reached the back of the property and looked out over the hill, she saw the door to the crypt open.

Josh emerged, stumbling in the direction of the cemetery gates just as the spirits crossed through, still dragging their victims, screaming behind them. Rachel knew they weren't going to catch up to the ghosts. As the crypt doors slammed closed again behind the entities and their victims, she skidded to a stop. Josh was now only a few feet away from them. Her heart pounded as he approached. Was it finally over?

She rushed the remaining few steps into Josh's arms and hugged him tight. Rachel was so happy to see that he was still alive that she nearly knocked him off his feet. He smiled lightly, and she felt his arms wrap around her body. They had never felt as good as they did at that moment.

"What happened to you?" Rachel asked.

Josh sighed. "Zach came out of nowhere and knocked me out with a shovel. Or at least I think it was a shovel. It's all a little hazy right now. He shoved me into the crypt so no one would find me, but when I came to, I could hear everything."

"So, you heard what they were planning to do?"

"Yes, but I couldn't do anything at first. I heard Zach say he was going to suffocate Becky and then move in on you as you grieved. I was the one they were going to try to pin it all on."

"Well, looks like that plan failed miserably," Grace said. "None of it matters now that they're gone and it's all over with."

"Thank goodness everything worked out, and they got what they deserved," Josh said.

As they all started to head back for the house, Rachel sensed something behind them. Turning around slowly, she instantly found the spirits of her mother and grandmother looking back at her. She smiled in return to their smiles. She knew they would finally be able to rest in peace. Now that Rachel and Becky were safe, they could move on to whatever was beyond the afterlife. Slowly, the spirits dissipated, and that was when she knew everything was over. She and her sister could finally move forward, and the estate was safe.

EPILOGUE

Rachel was smiling as she watched her sister set up the tripod with her phone attached to it. They were preparing to go live with their viewers for the first time in several months, and the excitement between them was immense. While they had shared most of what had happened with their followers, they were about to go public with all the information they had found. Becky quickly finished aligning the camera and sat down next to her. Seconds later, they were live.

"Hey, everyone, it's me, Becky. We're live right now, just as we promised. I'm here with my sister, who you should all know. For those of you who don't, this is Rachel."

"That's right, everybody. We're live, and it's about to get real. Now, it's been just over six months since we made our way to the estate, and it became ours. Needless to say, to those who follow us regularly, it's been a rocky road since."

Becky smiled. "Maybe so, but we're here now. We survived, and this is our story. Not only were things quite messy here, but we learned some things about our grandmother along the way. Through her journal, we're going to let you all know what she found out."

The twins chuckled and opened the journal. As wild as the story was that they were about to tell, it was all true. They took turns reading from the journal and explaining to the people who were watching the things that had happened over the years. It was only through Patricia's own investigative work that they were able to have any of the information. The man named Collin Hunter had actually been a drifter who had moved from town to town and preyed on the weak-minded women he could manipulate. After setting his sights on Jessica, things took a turn in his favor.

"Basically, what he wanted from Jessica wasn't much more than he would ask of his victims, but in the middle of trying to work his charm, they got drunk one night, and she admitted her dark secret."

"She told him she had killed Patricia's husband with poison and didn't even get rid of the evidence," Becky continued. "From what we have learned, she kept the syringe she used to kill the man. It didn't take Collin long to get his hands on it and start blackmailing Jessica."

Rachel sighed. "The man stole millions from her, though I can't say she didn't deserve to lose everything she had. Still, after he had drained her of all her savings and more, he set his sights on getting ahold of Patricia's money. She quickly became his next target and moved to the area and started the next part of his plan."

"Unfortunately, our mother, Amanda, fell for his charm first and quickly became smitten with the guy. He quickly used the relationship to take advantage of her."

"Years after she had left and come back home, he ended up getting close and used a drug to make her pass out."

"Basically, a roofie," Becky added.

"Exactly, and he took advantage of her again. Only this time, he got her pregnant. After leaving again and finding out she was pregnant, Amanda came back home in an attempt to tell her mother what had happened," Rachel said.

"Only problem was, Collin found out why she had come back, and he knew he had to stop her. Knowing he still had dirt on Jessica, he used that to blackmail her into helping him. She's the one who lured Amanda to the river under false pretenses, and she wasted no time shoving her in."

Rachel and her sister were overjoyed to see the amount of support they were getting in their comments and kept pushing forward with the story. It was difficult to talk about their mother and grandmother they never knew, but they had come from a strong background of women. Knowing what Patricia and Amanda had gone through was hard enough, but the more they talked and shared everything, the better she felt.

Rachel sighed. "Sadly, Patricia never knew about us until after Amanda's death. Things had happened so fast that our mother never got the chance to tell her before Jessica murdered her. Without any proof as to what Collin had done, she spent time learning all she could about the man."

"It didn't take long for her to stumble upon the clues that led her from Collin to Jessica. Soon after that, she learned that Zach was part of it, as well. Each one of them is behind some aspect of the murders. Patricia kept everything she found in her journal and wrote all that she learned about the three in it."

"As much as she wanted the world to know the truth and as hard as she tried to keep what she knew from the three killers, Patricia never got the chance to tell anyone before she, too, was killed."

Becky took a deep breath and smiled. "As hard as it was to learn that our family had gone through all of that, it's good to know they all received the justice they deserved. They were each sentenced recently, with Collin getting the heaviest and harshest punishment He won't be seeing the outside of a prison for the rest of his life."

As they finished their live feed to their viewers, Rachel happily let them all know the twins were going to be staying put. After everything they had endured in their lives, each of them knew the future was better where they were. The estate had quickly become their home, and they both shared the same dream of opening the estate to traveling artists in need of a break or a mysterious history lesson.

Either way, Rachel and Becky were happy things were finally coming together. After years of being on their own and traveling the country, they had a place they could call home. They finished off the feed by telling their viewers they loved them and thanked each of them for their support. Rachel was blowing kisses to their fans when Becky jumped up to turn off the phone.

Josh walked in at the same time, walked right up to Rachel, and wrapped her in his arms. She would never tire of his warm embrace, and she melted into the love he had for her. Things had never been better between the two, and she was happy to have the man in her life. He supported her in every way, and they were planning to marry by the end of the year.

Becky was taking care of almost everything on the website now, but Rachel didn't mind. It gave her much more time to plan for the estate's future and prepare for the upcoming wedding. Plus, the extra time she got to spend with Josh was well worth it.

As she thought about how great things were going for them, she couldn't help but think about how much better Grace was doing. The last time she had talked to the woman, she had called from Paris. It was the fourth international city she had visited, and Rachel was happy to see how well she was doing and how free Grace had become since she was no longer tied to Jessica.

Things were going better than she ever imagined they could be. Now that the twins had settled in to living at the estate, the sky was the limit for both of them. Rachel had sensed a peace the moment the spirits had finished their journey. She smiled as she thought about how the Red River Estate was finally at peace, and so was her family.

Made in United States
North Haven, CT
09 November 2024